I0732878

Hunting Romance

HOLLY S ROBERTS

WICKED STORY TELLING

Copyright © 2025 by Holly S Roberts

All rights reserved.

No part of this book may be reproduced, distributed, or transmitted in any form or by any means, including photocopying, recording, or other electronic or mechanical methods, without the prior written permission of the author, except in the case of brief quotations embodied in reviews and certain other noncommercial uses permitted by copyright law. This book and its contents may not be used, copied, stored, or processed by artificial intelligence (AI) systems, machine learning models, or any automated technology for the purposes of data mining, content generation, or derivative works without the express written consent of the author. Any unauthorized use by AI or similar technologies is strictly prohibited.

This book is a work of fiction. Names, characters, businesses, places, events, and incidents are either the products of the author's imagination or used fictitiously. Any resemblance to actual persons, living or dead, or actual events is purely coincidental.

Contents

Romance Titles

Completion Sports

Play

Goal

Strike

Kick

Ruck

Slam

Hotter Than Hell

Heat

Sizzle

Burn

Street Justice

Ignite

Combust

Prologue

Dear Ms. Bernard,

I am Peter Gilbrick of Michaels, Thane, and Gillbrick, LLP, and I represented your great uncle Anthony Gables. He passed away on January 4 of this year. We were given strict guidance not to inform you of his passing until several items were completed from the list he left in his will. Mr. Gables is now buried in the family plot on the east end of the property, though the headstone has not been ordered, so you and Mr. Callaway can decide what you want the headstone to say and how it will look.

I wish to inform you that your uncle left you and his butler's grandson, Jamie Callaway, his property and financial holdings. Mr. Hobbs, the butler, had died the year before Mr. Gables. We are aware you had no contact with Mr. Gables.

Jamie Callaway never met your uncle, and you are both in the same predicament.

There are several non-negotiable stipulations in the will that I will now cover.

First, you must live in his home with Jamie for one year. If at any time, either of you leaves the house separately for more than seventy-two hours, the person remaining behind inherits the majority of the estate, and the other receives a flat inheritance of $100,000. If you are together, the time away from the house is extended to ten days.

Second, during the year, all living expenses will be paid by the estate.

Third, you are vegan and write vegan cookbooks. Jamie Callaway is a hunting guide for large deadly carnivores. You will learn the way of the hunter, and Jamie will learn the way of the vegan. You will share your heartfelt reasons for your life choices, and he will share his. You will accompany him on hunts, though you are not required to physically harm an animal. Mr. Callaway will accompany you to places or events that helped convince you to partake of your lifestyle. While in the house, Mr. Callaway will eat only the vegan food you cook. Sneaking away for meals is not permitted. You may both eat whatever you wish while on hunting expeditions. When in the house, breakfast and dinner will be eaten together in the formal dining room.

The first person to arrive at the house on April 1 has the choice of the preferred bedroom. No major changes to the house are permitted until the year is up. If both you and Mr. Callaway accomplish the stipulations of the will, the house will be in both your names, and the remainder of the estate will be split equally between you.

I strongly suggest you give your notice at work immediately and make plans to start your new life. You will find more information on the following pages. Please let me know if you decide to forgo the inheritance and give it to Mr. Jamie Callaway in the next twenty-four hours.

Sincerely,

Peter Gilbrick

Michaels, Thane, and Gillbrick, LLP

Chapter One

DAVIS

She arrived early on April 1. Davis couldn't help wondering if the entire adventure was some kind of cosmic joke. The date said yes; her investigation said no.

The property surrounding the monstrosity of a house was overgrown with vegetation in varying shades of greens and browns, making it even more ominous or beautiful depending on how you looked at it. Surprisingly, Davis knew she could be at home here, where nature crept to the front door. She hadn't expected to have this instant connection, but the property called to her inner wild child.

The cold brass handle turned in her hand, and she stepped inside the dark, mysterious house. Nightlights made the room formally depressing. The overcast night or more correctly very early morning helped maintain the dreary feeling she'd had since she opened her eyes.

The letter from the attorney was tucked safely in her pocket. It gave her permission to enter, but she still felt like a burglar in a B-grade movie. She left her bags in the trunk of her beat-up car just in case. The large entryway with its stunning chandelier showcased the front room, and the size of the old house was rather intimidating. Her entire apartment would fit into the front room.

What the hell had she expected?

Not much. As soon as she received the attorney's letter, she called her mom and asked about her great uncle Anthony.

"I never met him, but from what your grandmother said, God rest her soul, he was a recluse and had nothing to do with the family."

She told her mother about the letter.

"Are you going to do it?" her mother asked with nervous laughter.

"I don't even know if it's real or some kind of practical joke," Davis replied.

"How would anyone know about your great uncle Anthony? You didn't even know about him."

"Why is that?" she asked.

"I never really thought about him. He was more of a rumor. Like I said, he wanted nothing to do with the family. Your grandmother said he had more money than God, but to me, that was also a rumor. I haven't thought about him in at least forty years."

"I'm inclined to believe the letter is real, but that doesn't mean I won't research it further. I'll start by looking up the law office and calling them to speak with Mr. Gilbrick directly."

"If the letter is true, just think of what you could do with the money. You've dreamed of having a farm animal rescue, and this would give you that dream."

"You're forgetting Mr. Callaway."

"Oh posh, if what your grandmother said was true, there's plenty of money for you both to live your dreams. I just hope he's not dangerous or anything."

As Davis's gaze scanned the slightly musty room, she thought about Jamie Callaway. She looked him up online and found an old photograph of him from a hunting expedition. He was standing beside a hunter who was lifting the mammoth head of a lion, and they were smiling into the camera. Her stomach had turned at the sight, and she hated Jamie Callaway before she even met him.

And what kind of person had no online presence? He wasn't on TikTok or any of the other apps. She detested the fact that she'd had to look on the right-wing sites to be sure he didn't have accounts there.

Nothing.

Other than the one image, where he was slightly out of focus with a face covered in hair, she found nothing. She couldn't even tell if he had serial killer eyes or not.

Now she would be living with the man for one year.

But first she wanted the master bedroom. A map of the house came with the attorney's letter. Only the main bedroom had an en-suite bathroom, and she'd be damned if she was going to walk down a hallway to pee.

She checked the time on her phone: 3:22 a.m. Her rival would arrive early for the room, so she had left her apartment eight hours ago and traveled through the night so he wouldn't win. This point would be hers.

She turned to the right and climbed the stairs, which circled around to a wide veranda that looked over the front room. Davis walked quickly to the end of the hall where double doors faced her.

With force, she pushed through the doors and froze in her tracks.

A naked man stood before her.

Bent over slightly with a towel in his hands, he dried his wet hair but glanced in her direction. Upside-down eyes stared at her. She only partially noticed because most of her attention was on the penis that dangled between his legs.

A rather large penis.

He slowly stood upright.

"Ms. Bernard, I presume?" he said with a thick, deep voice he didn't deserve.

Covering himself with the towel would have been the gentlemanly thing to do, but instead, he slapped it over his shoulder and turned to face her full-on.

"My eyes are up here," he said softly.

Could you literally fall through a floor? If you could, it needed to open up right now and suck her down.

Suck. Not a good word to think about at this moment.

"Ms. Bernard, or if you are not Ms. Bernard, tell me so I can call the police and tell them I have a voyeur in the house."

Her eyes snapped to his. "Voyeur?" she replied indignantly.

"If the shoe fits. And it is a rather large shoe, as you've observed."

The heat in her face went to a boil. The last thing she wanted to look like was a lobster to this meat eater.

"You thought you would beat me to the master bedroom, didn't you?" he said a little too cockily.

Cock. Another word she shouldn't think about.

Finally, she examined Jamie Callaway's facial features. The image she'd found did him no justice. He wasn't classically handsome because his nose was a little too large and his eyes a bit too in-set, but somehow it worked for him. The dark brown facial hair really needed to go, but even that didn't take away his delectable façade. What wasn't working for her was the desire to lick her lips.

"Yes, I'm Davis. And now that we have that formality behind us, could you cover yourself?"

"Why? You've seen it all. Maybe you would like me to turn around slowly so you can have the whole effect. I'll warn you, though, turnabout is fair play. Why don't you take off your clothes so I don't feel so naked."

He was embarrassing her on purpose, and her aggravation grew.

"Me being naked would do nothing to make you less so." What a neanderthal. "And yes, I thought I would arrive before you and acquire this room. Is there anything I can do to convince you to give it to me?"

"Take off your clothes," he said without a hint of playfulness in his eyes.

"You are reprehensible." She turned around and stormed from the room, slamming the door behind her.

What a complete asshole.

Chapter Two

JAMIE

Well, that was interesting. Jamie inhaled to regain his forgotten control and looked down. He'd felt the erection growing because, what the hell? Ms. Davis Bernard was gorgeous. He'd expected a middle-aged, pert-nosed, condescending bitch related to an old man who was unlikable for most of his life. Why wouldn't Davis be the same?

Okay, the bitch part was still debatable, and he would take the time to make up his mind. As far as being middle-aged, she was far off that mark. She looked younger than him by at least a few years. Davis didn't have a pert nose because hers was perfect, and the rest of her face was as classically beautiful as her nose. And her hair. It could almost be classified as fire-engine red. But for all that was holy, her lips were her crowning glory: full, luscious, and entirely kissable.

Did vegans kiss?

He'd looked up veganism and almost gagged at the information he found on his favorite carnivore sites. Davis didn't look like she was dying of protein and iron deficiency, but from everything he read, the lack of key nutrients, whatever those were, made her crazy. It also meant she would have a hard time keeping up while trekking on a hunt. Maybe he could lose her easily and pick her up on his way out of the forest. Doing so would most likely place her life in danger because vegans knew nothing about the wilds.

Now that the horrors of her diet were imprinted on his brain, tofu held the lead on disgusting. Tofu, for fuck's sake. The vegan weirdos didn't even eat cheese or drink milk. How could any sane person survive?

Unfortunately, he was about to find out. He'd arrived at midnight to make sure he got the best room, and for that, he would pay. Her counterplay would be to make the most disgusting vegan meal imaginable. And how did he know this? It's what he would do. It would be something like lettuce wraps with nothing but green, mushy shit inside.

He hated mushy shit along with anything green. He'd had an aversion to vegetables since he was a child, and he didn't plan on getting over it. But hell, those lips. Sitting across from her at a table each night would not be difficult.

Food would be the hardest part of this challenge. He loved to eat; it was one of his extravagances. While traveling, which he did a lot, he found the best restaurants. Some were five-star; some were holes in the wall with the greatest food served anywhere. His taste for fine cuisine was the one thing that overshadowed his love for the hunt.

His friends didn't understand. They thought he had the best job ever—a career for real men: the great outdoors and the chance to pit oneself against the mightiest beasts man could go up against. Jamie let them have their illusions.

What he actually did was take a bunch of pampered men with too much money on an adventure where he did all the work and collected none of the glory. These men wanted to pretend they were part of nature until the first mosquito bite.

His last expedition had two brothers who never stopped bickering with each other and complained about the elements constantly. His next hunt, the one Davis would be on, involved friends of those brothers, and he expected them to be just as bad.

He rubbed his hands together. The next hunt would be a classic.

He shook his head, partly to clear it, partly because everything about Davis Bernard short-circuited the common-sense portion of his brain. He hadn't expected her to walk in on him naked, though he also wasn't exactly sorry about it. He also hadn't expected the way she'd looked at him: like she hated him, and maybe wanted to lick him, and also wanted to bury him alive in the vegetable garden she'd inevitably plant.

Contradictions. All wrapped up in one gorgeous, furious, red-haired vegan.

He dropped the towel on the bed and pulled on a pair of sweats. No shirt, just so he could annoy her. If he was forced to eat tofu for the foreseeable future, he could at least enjoy the small victories.

Padding downstairs, he followed the faint sounds of cabinets opening and closing. She was already in the kitchen, pretending to take inventory while actually planning revenge. He paused in the doorway.

Davis stood at the massive farmhouse sink, shoulders stiff, her hair shoved into a messy bun that somehow made her look like a pissed-off Disney heroine. She'd found a cleaning rag and was aggressively scrubbing the counter as if it had personally wronged her.

He leaned against the doorframe. "Should I be worried about the safety of the pots and pans?"

She didn't look at him. "Only if they make sexist comments about my clothes."

He grinned. "Fair enough. Though for the record, I wasn't commenting on your clothes. Mostly because you were fully dressed, which seemed unfair."

She froze, rag suspended mid-wipe. "Jamie?"

"Mhm?"

She turned slowly, like a woman preparing to face a firing squad. "I'm going to say this once. I am not your enemy. I don't want to fight every minute we're in this house."

"Great," he said. "Then don't walk into my room unannounced."

Her eyebrows shot up. "It was going to be my room."

"You snooze, you lose." He pointed at his chest. "In this case, literally."

Her mouth opened, then shut again, like she had too many insults and couldn't pick just one. Finally, she tossed the rag on the counter.

"Fine. Whatever. We have twelve months. We will set boundaries so we don't kill each other."

"Okay," he said easily. "Boundary one: no looking at my dick unless you ask nicely."

The sound she made defied categorization. It was part outrage, part mortification, part maybe admiration. "I didn't look at," she stopped, then tried again. "You were, I mean," another hesitation. "I walked in on. Oh my God."

He laughed. Couldn't help it. Watching her flustered was far better than watching her furious.

She crossed her arms tightly over her chest. "Serious boundaries."

He held up both hands in surrender. "Shoot."

"Rule one," she said. "Knocking. Always. No exceptions."

"Done."

"Rule two: absolutely no, what's the word, ogling?"

"Is that what you were doing? Good to know."

Her glare could have melted steel. "I mean, you don't get to ogle me."

"Oh, sweetheart," he drawled, "you're walking around in yoga pants and righteous indignation. I'm only human."

She sputtered, gripping the countertop like she needed the stability. "Rule three," she said tightly. "Meals. The will said we eat together. Fine. But you will not complain about my cooking."

"I will if it tastes like sadness, betrayal, or shit."

Her face turned red, but she bit back what she was first going to say. "It won't," she settled on.

"You don't know that." He really enjoyed pushing her buttons.

"I do," she snapped. "Because unlike some people, I know how to cook."

"Shots fired," he said with a low whistle.

"Last rule," she continued, ignoring him. "No sabotaging each other. No tricking, no trapping, no sneaking meat into my pantry, and no trying to lose me in a forest."

He lifted his brows. "You think I'd actually do that?"

"Yes."

Fair.

She exhaled sharply through her nose. "Now. I'm going to bring in my suitcases. Try to resist being obnoxious after I get back."

He watched her stomp out the side door, the sway of her hips unintentionally hypnotic. Maybe he'd underestimated vegans. Maybe he'd underestimated himself too.

He wandered into the walk-in pantry, scanning shelves overflowing with ingredients he couldn't identify. What the hell was nutritional yeast? And why did she have four bags of it? It sounded like a female vaginal infection. He had sisters and he unfortunately knew about these things. What was Davis planning? A cult initiation?

He grabbed a jar, squinted at the label, and muttered, "Chia seeds? Sounds like something you feed birds."

"They're good for you," came her voice behind him.

He hadn't heard her come back in. He turned to see her hauling a massive suitcase up the last step, breathing hard.

"Your protein intake is too low," he said confidently.

She dropped the suitcase with a thud that made the floorboards protest. "I can deadlift more than you think."

"Impressive. But can you cook something edible? That's the real test."

She rolled the suitcase past him. "Challenge accepted."

A warning chill ran down his spine. He wasn't sure what she'd make, but he was suddenly very sure it would prove some kind of point of which he was the target.

"Dinner at six," she declared. "I'm exhausted and plan on sleeping through breakfast. Don't be late."

"I won't," he said. "Wouldn't want to miss your attempt to poison me with," he looked down at the name on the new bag he'd picked up, "legumes."

She paused in the doorway, turning slowly. A slow, dangerous smile curved her lips.

"Oh Jamie," she said sweetly, "you have no idea what you're in for."

And damn it. He couldn't wait.

Chapter Three

JAMIE

He showed up at 5:59 p.m., not because he wanted to be punctual, but because he wanted her to know he *could* be punctual.

He leaned against the dining room doorway; arms crossed over his bare chest. He hadn't bothered with a shirt again. She hadn't said anything about his bare chest earlier in the kitchen, but he knew it bothered her. Eyes didn't lie, and she liked what she saw. His new mission was to annoy her at every turn.

The room, with its high ceilings and antique chandelier, looked like it belonged in some historical drama. It only made him appear more out of place. He felt like a wild animal trapped in a museum.

From the kitchen drifted a smell he could only describe as green. Grassy. Earth-adjacent. His stomach tightened with the dread of a man approaching his execution.

Davis swept into the dining room, carrying a large platter. She'd changed into a black tank top and loose linen pants, and her hair was flowing freely down her back like she was auditioning for cottage-core porn.

He hated that she was stunning and damned sexy. It was deeply inconvenient.

She set the platter on the table with a flourish and rested it between two lit candles.

Jamie stared at it.

"Oh hell no."

The dish looked like a pile of green patties. What did you call these? Fritters? Puck-shaped shit, though they smelled faintly of garlic.

She smiled. "Dinner."

"What is it?" he asked cautiously.

"Spinach-lentil cakes with cashew cream sauce."

"Those are words, sure," he said, "but they don't go together to form food."

She pulled out her chair with regal grace. "Sit, Jamie."

He narrowed his eyes. "Why do I feel like this is step one of the cult?"

"Sit," she repeated, enunciating each letter.

He sat. Mostly because refusing meant losing to her, and that was unacceptable.

She served him two green patties, drowning them in white sauce. He stared at the plate like it might lunge with octopus legs and suck the life from him.

"Is this revenge for earlier?" he asked.

"Earlier?" she said innocently, cutting into her meal. "You'll have to be more specific. Was it the 'take off your clothes' comment? Or the ogling rule? Or the accusation that my diet is, what was your phrase? Oh. 'Sadness, betrayal and shit.'"

He winced. "Okay, I deserved that."

"Eat," she said, like a command given by a queen to a peasant.

Jamie picked up his fork. Hesitated. Eyed her.

She raised one brow. "Do you need an airplane sound to help get the fork into your mouth?"

He stabbed a spinach-lentil cake with unnecessary aggression. "I can feed myself, thanks."

"Prove it."

He took a bite.

And paused.

Chewed.

Paused again.

Davis leaned forward, elbows on the table. "Well?"

"It doesn't taste like dirt," he admitted.

She smirked. "High praise."

He took another bite. "It's actually not terrible."

She put a hand to her chest in mock emotion. "Oh my gosh. That is the nicest thing you have ever said to me."

"I said you were gorgeous."

She blinked. "When?"

"In my head." He swallowed. "I'm saying it now: You're gorgeous."

Her fork clattered onto her plate. "Jamie."

"What? I'm not blind." He swallowed. "And these patties of virtue are better than expected. Don't get cocky."

"I'm not cocky," she said, recovering her composure. "I'm just pleasantly surprised you have functioning taste buds."

He picked up the sauce carafe. "What's this white stuff again? Cashew something?"

"Cashew cream."

"You milked a nut," he said flatly.

She burst into laughter so suddenly that he forgot to breathe for a second.

"Oh my God," she choked out. "Jamie please, never say that again."

He grinned. "Why? It's accurate."

"It's horrifying," she said, wiping tears from her eyes. "And inaccurate."

"It's only horrifying because cashews don't have nipples," he argued.

"They don't need them!"

"Everything needs nipples," he shot back.

"No, everything does not," she insisted.

"Fine, name one thing that doesn't need nipples." He crossed his arms in pure smugness.

"You're incorrigible," she said, trying not to smile, but he saw the corners of her incredible lips turn up. "Fine. Fire hydrants," she said at last.

"Not the direction I expected, but okay," he conceded, then didn't say anything for a moment. "Now that I've thought about it, liquid does come out of the hydrant when you milk it."

She tossed her napkin at him, and he burst out laughing.

They kept eating, the joking easing into a comfortable rhythm that surprised them both. Jamie found himself taking a third then a forth patty. Davis pretended not to notice, but she absolutely noticed and was glowing with smug satisfaction.

He surprisingly liked the food, even though he knew he would be protein-deficient until he ate some of the jerky he'd left in his car, which was parked in the large garage. There was nothing in the will about sneaking to his car to take advantage of required protein and iron, he just couldn't bring it into the house or drive somewhere to pick some up. He'd brought a very large supply.

Halfway through the meal, thunder rolled outside. The power flickered.

Davis glanced toward the window. "A storm's coming in."

Jamie nodded. "Old houses always make storms sound worse."

Right on cue, a loud creak echoed through the house.

Davis jumped, then immediately tried to hide it by sipping her water.

"Scared?" Jamie teased.

"No," she lied.

Another thunderclap shook the windows. She flinched again.

Jamie bit back a smile. "You want me to check the house? Make sure no murderers have gotten in?"

"No one is in this house except us."

He tilted his head. "You sure? It's huge. Lots of dark corners. Could be a ghost. Or, worse," he lowered his voice dramatically, "a cow seeking revenge for your childhood decision to go vegan. He could have had a good death at the slaughterhouse, and you took that away from him."

She threw a piece of spinach at him. "Shut up."

He chuckled. "Fine. I'll protect you."

"I don't need protecting."

Crash.

Somewhere upstairs, something large fell over.

Davis stood so fast her chair scraped. "Okay, maybe I need protecting a little."

Jamie rose, stretching languidly like a cat who enjoyed its own power.

She crossed her arms. "We're just going to look. Nothing more."

"Of course," he said, picking up a candlestick like a medieval weapon. "Ladies first."

"No," she said immediately. "You first."

"Thought you didn't need protecting."

"Jamie. Move."

He grinned and stepped towards the stairs.

And somehow, without either of them saying it, they walked up together, close enough their arms brushed, into whatever the old house had waiting for them.

Chapter Four

DAVIS

His shirtless chest was too much. Much too much. She wanted to stop him on the stairs and run her fingers over each rope of muscle. That would be bad.

The stairs groaned under their weight. It was like they resented being awakened by two idiots who didn't understand self-preservation. Jamie walked ahead of her, holding a brass candlestick like it was Excalibur, and she couldn't decide if she wanted to shove him, hide behind him, or rub against him.

Preferably all of the above.

Another low rumble of thunder rolled through the house. She pretended she didn't jump. He pretended not to notice, which she appreciated.

What kind of house made noises like this?

Large, old, probably haunted ones. The kind where someone died mysteriously in 1923 and then stuck around because they couldn't let go of their favorite armchair.

They reached the landing. The upstairs hallway stretched out too long, too dark, too, queue horror-movie-opening-scene. The lights flickered, because of course they did. This place was cliché enough to be self-aware.

Jamie glanced over his shoulder. "Still okay back there?"

"I'm fine."

Lie.

He smirked like he could smell her anxiety. "You're gripping the banister like you're trying to strangle it."

She loosened her fingers immediately. "I'm just being cautious."

"Mm-hmm." He raised his makeshift weapon. "Well, stay close. I don't want to have to explain to a lawyer how my roommate was eaten by a ghost."

"I don't think ghosts eat people."

"Have you met this house? I doubt it has vegan ghosts." He started walking again.

She followed, glaring at the back of his stupidly broad shoulders. Damnit, bare shoulders. Why did he look like that? Why did muscles exist? Why did *her* brain react to said muscles like it had been lobotomized?

Not the time or place, Davis, she told herself.

They approached the end of the hallway where the thud had come from. A faint draft brushed her ankles. The house breathed. Or exhaled. Or sighed the sigh of a place that really needed therapy.

Jamie reached the door to a spare bedroom and tried the knob. It turned easily.

He pushed it open slowly.

The room was dark except for the faint gray storm-light seeping through the curtains. Furniture loomed like shadow monsters. A painting on the far wall hung crookedly, swaying slightly.

She clutched Jamie's arm before she could stop herself.

He froze.

Oh God. She touched him. She had touched the shirtless hunter man. Her palm was directly on his warm, solid bicep.

She yanked her hand back like he was a hot stove.

"Sorry," she whispered.

He didn't turn around. "You're fine."

His voice rumbled low, and something traitorous fluttered in her stomach.

Focus, Davis. You are not flirting with a carnivore who thinks vegetables are optional.

Jamie stepped farther into the room. Something crunched under his foot.

He crouched, lifted what looked like a small, framed photograph from the floor, and showed it to her.

"Fell off the dresser," he said. "Probably the storm."

The glass hadn't shattered, just popped out. The frame was old, gold leaf peeling slightly, the photo inside black-and-white and faded. A man in a stiff suit stared somewhere off-camera, expression stern, like someone had just informed him joy was illegal.

"Your great uncle?" Jamie asked.

"I don't know." She took the frame from him, tracing the worn edge. "The attorney didn't send pictures of him."

Jamie brushed past her, moving to the window. He pulled the curtains aside. The latch was loose; the wind had pushed it open a crack.

"That's probably all it was," he said. "Storm pressure rattling things."

She exhaled, tension slowly bleeding out. "So, no ghosts?"

He shrugged. "Didn't say that."

She scowled. "Would you please not?"

"Not what?"

"Add unnecessary fear gaslighting into the moment."

His mouth twitched. "Fear gaslighting? Is that a vegan thing too?"

"It's a human thing, you barbarian."

He chuckled, then fiddled with the latch until it clicked shut.

Another boom of thunder made her flinch so hard she hit the dresser behind her.

Jamie turned fully. His eyes softened in a way she wasn't prepared for.

"Hey," he said gently, "you okay?"

"Yes."

Lie number two.

"You sure?"

"Jamie," she said through clenched teeth, "thunder is loud, and this house sounds like it's trying to confess to murder. I'm allowed to flinch."

He stepped closer. Not touching her. But close enough that his warmth wrapped around her like a blanket she didn't ask for but kind of wanted.

"We can head back downstairs," he said softly. "Nothing's up here except some crooked art and your creepy ancestor."

She huffed a laugh. "He does look like he hates joy."

"Hates shirtless men more, probably."

She rolled her eyes. "Everyone hates shirtless men."

"No," he said with quiet confidence, "they don't."

Was he flirting?

No. Impossible.

Absolutely not.

Except, maybe?

Thunder cracked again. Instinctively again she stepped closer to him.

And he didn't make a joke this time. Didn't tease. Just stayed steady, letting her pretend she hadn't just used him as a human emotional support mountain.

"Come on," he said finally. "Let's get downstairs. Maybe heat up some tea."

She blinked. "You drink tea?"

"No," he admitted. "But you do. And I think you need something warm before the house decides to make another dramatic noise."

For one horrifying second, she felt gratitude. Real gratitude.

He gestured toward the hall, letting her walk ahead.

"Jamie," she said, stopping in the doorway, "thank you. For, you know. Not being horrible for five minutes."

He smirked. "Don't get used to it."

"Believe me, I won't."

But as they walked back toward the warm glow of the dining room, the storm growling outside, she couldn't shake the feeling that something had shifted.

Just a little.

Barely noticeable.

But undeniably there.

Chapter Five

JAMIE

He smelled breakfast before he saw it. The aroma confused Jamie's brain on a molecular level. On one hand, it smelled good: warm, savory, and comforting. On the other hand, he somehow knew tofu was involved, which meant something treacherous was lurking beneath the pleasantness.

He stepped into the kitchen shirtless again, because consistency mattered, rubbing the sleep from his eyes. Davis stood at the stove in soft gray shorts and an oversized sweatshirt, her braid messy and low. She looked maddeningly domestic. Domestic enough that he had a fleeting, horrifying thought:

Is this what a wife looks like?

He immediately shut that thought down.

"Morning," she said without turning. "Coffee's ready."

He blinked. "You drink coffee?"

"Only when I have to deal with hunters."

Fair.

He poured himself a mug and took a sip. It was strong enough to revive a corpse. He liked it.

His gaze drifted to the stove. There were two pans. One was filled with diced potatoes crisping to a golden brown; the other containing, he squinted.

Something white. Something yellowish. Something green?

He pointed. "That looks like eggs, but I know it's not eggs."

"It's not eggs," she confirmed.

"It wants to be eggs."

"It's not trying to be anything."

"It's tofu pretending to be eggs."

She sighed, long-suffering. "It's tofu medley with turmeric, kale, onion, and garlic. It's delicious."

He leaned against the counter, arms crossed. "We'll see."

She plated the potatoes, then the tofu mixture, and finally sliced into a loaf of thick sourdough bread she'd brought in from her car last night.

He watched her cut it.

He watched her way too intently.

"Is that home-baked?" he asked.

"Yes."

"As in, you made it?"

She gave him a look. "That's what homemade means."

"It smells," his pride tried to stop him, but truth pushed through, "incredible."

Her expression flickered: surprise, then pride, then her usual Davis-armor slid back into place. "Thank you," she said softly.

She brought the plates to the table. "Sit. Eat. Complain after."

He sat. Picked up his fork. Poked the tofu with suspicion.

Davis raised an eyebrow. "Are you going to interrogate it first?"

"Yes. I need to understand its motives."

She rolled her eyes so hard she might've sprained something. "Just taste it."

He did.

And he didn't immediately want to spit it out.

He took another bite.

And another.

It was actually good. A little spicy. The potatoes were crispy perfection, and the bread.

Holy hell, the bread.

He chewed slowly, trying not to show emotion. He was a bachelor who visited high-end restaurants but did not get home-cooked meals.

Davis watched him with the smugness of a woman awaiting a verdict she already knew.

"Well?" she finally asked.

Jamie set down his fork. "I hate this."

She frowned. "Why?"

"Because I like it."

Her grin was immediate. Victorious. Satisfying for reasons he didn't want to examine.

"Told you," she said, taking a sip of her coffee. "Tofu is not the enemy."

"It is absolutely the enemy. It just has a good PR team today."

Her foot bumped his under the table. Accidentally, he figured, but they both froze for a fraction of a second before pretending it didn't happen.

She cleared her throat. "Anyway. Plans for the day."

He finished chewing a bite of bread that deserved its own religion. "Yeah. I was thinking we check out the property.

Make sure nothing's fallen, no trees blocking paths. The forest is thick out there."

"I'd like to see the greenhouse," she said. "The attorney mentioned one."

He nodded. "It's behind the house. Probably a mess. This place hasn't been maintained for, what? Months?"

"Feels like years," she muttered.

"What else?" he asked.

"I want to explore the attic," she said. "There's always cool stuff in attics: old trunks, creepy portraits, antique diaries that definitely aren't haunted."

"Davis," he said deadpan, "the attic is one hundred percent haunted."

She pointed her fork at him. "Don't start."

"Storm last night, house older than Moses, drafty halls. Yeah, something up there wants to eat our souls."

"You're not funny."

"I'm hilarious."

"Debatable."

He smirked. "We can check the attic after we walk the property. Daylight seems wise. You spooked pretty easily last night."

She bristled. "I did not."

"You grabbed my arm so hard I lost circulation."

"That was one time!"

"And it was adorable."

Her mouth fell open. "Take it back."

"Nope."

"You're impossible."

"Thank you."

She scowled at him, but her cheeks were pink.

"We also need to go through the file the attorney left," she said, redirecting the conversation with more force than necessary. "See what counts as 'major changes' to the house."

"No tearing down walls," Jamie said. "Or painting the place pink."

"Why would I paint it pink?"

"Because you're a woman."

She gave him a slow, deadly look. "Say that again."

He lifted his hands in surrender. "I'm kidding, calm down."

"You are insufferable."

"And you're predictable."

"Excuse me?"

"You look like someone who organizes her spices alphabetically."

She did. She absolutely did. She stabbed another bite of medley. "Let's just focus on the property. We walk the grounds. We take a look at the greenhouse. Then the attic. Then maybe we tackle the kitchen cabinets."

"You mean the cabinets filled with things like chia seeds and nutritional yeast?"

"Those are staples!"

"Those are bird food."

She sighed dramatically. "I should've let the storm take you."

He chuckled, pushing back from the table as he finished the last of his potatoes. "You ready?"

She stood, grabbing their plates. "Give me five minutes to change."

"Into what?" he asked. "A hazmat suit? In case we run into non-organic fertilizer?"

She tossed her napkin at him without turning. "Into shoes, Jamie. Shoes."

He grinned, raising his mug. As she disappeared upstairs, he couldn't deny the absurd truth warming his chest. He was actually looking forward to spending the day with her.

Even if she fed him tofu again.

Chapter Six

DAVIS

The early afternoon sun drifted through the tall trees surrounding the property, casting shifting patterns of gold and shadow across the grass. Davis walked beside Jamie, arms folded, trying to decide whether she was irritated, or simply overwhelmed by the sheer size of the estate.

Probably both.

Jamie strode across the overgrown path like he'd been born in the wilderness. He carried a small hatchet. "Just in case," he'd said, which she suspected was more for effect than necessity. She refused to let him see her appreciate how obnoxiously competent he looked.

"So," he said, glancing at her, "on a scale from one to ten, how scared are you of the woods?"

"I hike," she said.

"That's not what I asked."

"Fine. Three."

"You jumped to a three awfully fast."

"Three is generous."

He grinned, sunlight catching the edges of his beard. "I'll try to get you to a five by the end of the day."

"I swear to God, Jamie, if you hide behind a tree and growl—"

"Oh, you'd know it was me. A real predator wouldn't give you a warning."

She stopped walking. "You did not just say that."

He shrugged, unapologetic. "You signed up to learn the way of the hunter. Think of this as your first lesson."

Her jaw clenched. "Lesson one: you're insufferable?"

He chuckled and kept walking, pushing aside a branch for her as they moved deeper into the property. She stepped under it reluctantly, annoyed that he'd thought to do something considerate before she could reject the gesture.

The trail opened into a quiet clearing. Tall grass swayed. Wildflowers dotted the landscape. Beyond it stood a long, weathered structure of glass and iron: the greenhouse.

"Oh," she breathed, the sight unexpectedly softening her.

Jamie followed her gaze. "Huh. Looks like a horror movie set."

"It's beautiful," she said.

"It's one wind gust away from collapse."

Davis walked ahead of him, heart lifting with each step. She pressed her hand to the old iron frame. The glass was dusty but intact. A few panes were cracked, spiderwebbed with lines like frozen lightning.

Inside, she could see shapes: plants long dead, tables strewn with rusted tools, a large ceramic pot tipped on its side.

She pushed the door. It groaned but swung inward.

Warm, stale air hit her. Jamie entered behind her, ducking his head.

"Well," she whispered, "it's got potential."

"It's got black mold," he countered.

She knelt near a cracked planter, touching the dry soil. "This could be a full vegetable garden. Herbs, tomatoes, cucumbers..."

"Let me guess," Jamie said, "all the ingredients for your tofu creations."

She looked up at him. "Yes. And maybe one day you'll grow up and appreciate real food."

"I appreciate real food. It just usually has a pulse."

She made a face. "Disgusting."

He grinned and continued scanning the greenhouse. "There's a door in the back."

Together they walked toward it. The wood had swollen with moisture; Jamie had to shoulder it open. Beyond it was a tiny potting room with a workbench covered in old seed packets. She ran her fingers across them, brushing away dust.

"Look," she said, holding up a packet faded with age. "Heirloom tomatoes. My uncle must've used these."

He leaned one hip against the bench. "What are heirloom tomatoes?"

"Old varieties."

"So, wrinkled tomatoes."

She sighed. "Everything is a joke to you, isn't it?"

He studied her for a moment, something unreadable flickering in his eyes. "Not everything."

Her stomach fluttered. It wasn't attraction, she told herself firmly, just surprise. Surprise and something else.

"We should check the rest of the property," she said quickly. "And the attic before it gets dark."

Jamie smirked. "Afraid of the attic in the dark?"

"Yes," she said without hesitation. "I value my life."

He laughed loudly, and she found herself smiling despite her best efforts.

The attic door was in the hallway near the master bedroom. The room that was his though she refused to acknowledge the possessive irritation that still sparked when she remembered seeing him naked in it.

Jamie pulled the string that released the folding ladder. It clattered down with a puff of dust and an ominous creak.

"Oh great," Davis muttered. "A ladder that hates us."

"You're going up first," he said.

"Absolutely not."

"You have the flashlight."

She held up the small flashlight from the kitchen drawer. "We can trade."

"I'm carrying the heavy stuff," he said, lifting a toolbox he'd grabbed from the mudroom purely to assert dominance over inanimate objects or so she guessed.

"Fine," she grumbled, climbing the ladder slowly. "But if something touches me, I will scream."

"Try not to," he said. "I don't want to fall off the ladder and die before I get my half of the estate."

She reached the top and stepped into the attic. And froze. It was massive.

Wooden beams stretched across the high ceiling. Boxes, trunks, old furniture, and covered shapes lined both sides. Dust motes floated in the light from the small, round window at the far end.

"It's," she whispered, "beautiful."

Jamie climbed up behind her, looking around. "It's a death trap."

"It's history."

"It's tetanus."

She ignored him and walked deeper into the space, flashlight beam dancing over stacks of books, vintage suitcases, and old sheet-draped portraits that leaned against the wall.

One portrait caught her eye. She lifted the sheet.

A man stared back. Stern, unsmiling, eyes dark and piercing met hers.

The same man from the fallen picture in the bedroom.

"Your great uncle," she teased.

"Not by blood," Jamie said as he stepped next to her, shoulder brushing hers. "Looks like someone who haunts hallways for fun."

She elbowed him lightly. "Stop. He *was* my family."

"Your cranky family."

She bit back a smile.

Then, something shifted.

A soft thud toward the far end of the attic. Not loud, but unusual.

Davis grabbed Jamie's arm instinctively. Again.

He glanced down at her hand, then at her.

"I thought we talked about this," he said.

"I'm not doing it on purpose," she whispered.

"I didn't say it was a problem."

The attic air suddenly felt warmer.

Too warm.

Jamie gently disentangled her fingers from his arm. "Stay here. I'll check."

"No," she said, straightening her posture as dignity slowly returned. "We go together."

He hesitated, then nodded. "Together."

They walked slowly toward the sound. The beam of light trembled only slightly in her hand.

At the end of the attic was an old trunk. Its lid had fallen shut, probably the source of the noise.

Jamie nudged it with his foot. "Just gravity."

Davis exhaled shakily. "Okay. Good."

Jamie looked at her again, expression softer than she'd ever seen on him.

"You know," he said, "you did pretty well."

"Pretty well?" she demanded. "I was brave."

He smirked. "You grabbed me again."

"It was instinct."

"Instinct to grab me."

"Oh my God." She pushed past him. "We're done here."

But as she climbed down the ladder ahead of him, heart hammering, she couldn't deny it:

There was something about exploring dark, creaking spaces with Jamie Callaway that made the world feel oddly safer.

Infuriatingly safer.

And she wasn't ready to think about why.

Chapter Seven

JAMIE

Ten days of tofu, chickpeas, unfamiliar leafy things, and bread so good it probably violated several federal regulations. Ten days of Davis Bernard's voice echoing through the halls, Davis's humming in the kitchen, Davis's infuriatingly perfect eyebrows lifting every time he said something "barbaric."

Ten days, and somehow the house didn't feel as spacious anymore.

Jamie knelt beside the large duffel bag he kept in the mudroom. It was the one he used for expeditions, and he began going through his gear. He always did this the day before a hunt: inventory, reorganize, repack, repeat. Routine calmed him. Routine made sense.

Unlike other things.

He pulled out the usual supplies: GPS tracker, first-aid kit, maps, satellite phone, rope, compact field-stove, extra ammunition, water filtration system. Everything about hunting was stabilizing.

Nothing like living with Davis.

He rubbed a hand across the back of his neck, stretching the muscles there. He hadn't slept great. He wasn't nervous about the hunt itself. He'd guided more trips than he could count. But taking Davis into the wilderness?

That made his stomach tighten.

She wasn't fragile, not even close, but she was inexperienced, stubborn, and deeply committed to not dying via cougar attack. Admirable, but not entirely realistic.

He packed the last item and stood, reaching for the faded green T-shirt draped over the back of the chair. He pulled it on thoughtlessly, distracted by mentally running through tomorrow's route, the weather forecast, and her probable reactions to bug bites.

He was adjusting the hem when he heard footsteps behind him.

"Holy cow," Davis said in a tone that made him turn.

She stood in the doorway with a mug of tea, blinking at him like he'd sprouted antlers.

"What?" he asked.

She took a slow sip before replying. "You're wearing a shirt."

He glanced down at himself. "And?"

"And in the ten days I've known you, you've basically been allergic to shirts. I was starting to think it was a personality trait."

"It's cold," he said defensively.

She arched a brow. "The thermostat is set to seventy-two."

"I'm acclimating to tomorrow's weather."

"It's going to be sixty-eight."

"Still acclimating."

She leaned against the doorframe, hiding a smile behind her mug. "Wow. And here I was thinking you put it on by accident."

He crossed his arms. "I didn't put it on by accident."

"You did," she said, delighted. "You one hundred percent did."

He ran a hand through his hair. "Davis—"

"Please don't take it off," she said, lifting a finger. "Let me enjoy this rare moment of seeing the elusive Jamie Callaway in his natural cotton-covered state."

He gave her a look. "Would you prefer I take it off?"

Her lips parted slightly. Not enough to be surprised, but enough to register that she absolutely had imagined him shirtless again.

She recovered quickly. "No. Leave it on. It's nice."

Nice?

He should not be this aware of her saying that.

"So," she said, clearing her throat and walking past him into the room, "is all that what you're bringing tomorrow?"

He nodded. "Yeah. Basic gear. Extra supplies because you're coming."

She narrowed her eyes. "That sounded like an insult."

"It wasn't." It was a little. He picked up the small satellite unit. "There's no cell service where we're going. This keeps us in contact in case anything happens."

"Anything like what?" she asked suspiciously.

"Animal encounters gone wrong, getting turned around, weather shifts." He paused. "You falling into a ravine."

She exhaled sharply. "I'm not falling into a ravine."

"Everyone thinks that right up until it happens."

"I am not everyone."

"I noticed," he said before he could catch himself.

Her expression softened. Just a flicker. Then she brushed hair behind her ear. "What time are we leaving?"

"Five."

"In the morning?" she asked, horrified.

"No, at night. Yes, in the morning."

She groaned. "That's barely a time. That's only a wisp of essence."

He smirked along with rolling his eyes. "You'll live."

"I might not," she muttered, sipping her tea. "You haven't seen me before caffeine."

"Oh, I've seen you before caffeine."

"That wasn't me. That was a demon possessing my body."

He chuckled. "I've handled worse."

"You've never handled me," she said without thinking and then froze.

He choked on his own breath. "What?"

She blinked. "I meant you've never handled someone like me. Ugh, no, I didn't, forget I said that."

Her cheeks flushed pink. He filed that image away for later.

She lifted her mug a little higher, defensive now. "Anyway. I'll be ready by five. Or five-ish. Five-oh-eight, perhaps."

"Five," he repeated.

"Five-oh-two."

"Five."

She huffed. "Fine."

He zipped the duffel. "We'll go slow. You stick close. Don't wander off."

"Why would I wander off?"

"Because you get curious," he said simply.

She opened her mouth to argue and then shut it again.

He had her. Victory tasted almost as good as her sourdough.

She crossed her arms. "You're assuming I'll be lost and helpless."

"No," he said, meeting her eyes. "I'm assuming I'll be responsible for you."

"Right," she murmured. "Well. Try not to be insufferable about it."

"No promises."

She rolled her eyes and turned to leave. "By the way," she said over her shoulder, "you should wear shirts more often."

He blinked. "Why?"

"Because," she said, pausing in the doorway with a hint of mischief, "it makes you easier to ignore."

Then she walked away.

Jamie stood alone in the mudroom, pulse annoyingly elevated, staring down at the shirt he had, in fact, put on by accident.

He wasn't sure what the hell tomorrow would bring.

But he knew one thing for certain:

He was not getting through this hunt unscathed.

Not by the wilderness.

Not by her.

Chapter Eight

JAMIE

Davis carried a bright pink backpack, stuffed to the brim, with a rainbow pony patch on the front. Where she got it, Jamie had no idea. She did it to irritate him, and it worked.

"Do you like it?" she asked when they met beside his car before leaving.

He simply stared.

"I get it," she said. "It will be hard to blend into my surroundings, but really that's the idea. The mountain lions will run when they see me coming, even though pink is not an aggressive color."

"It is now," he said under his breath.

They barely spoke during the six-hour drive to the rendezvous point.

The brothers were already waiting when Jamie and Davis pulled up to the trailhead.

Of course they were. Anthony and Trevor Fields were the type of men who showed up early so they could tell everyone they'd been waiting. Jamie had figured this out during one of many correspondences this past month.

Anthony, the elder, wore camouflage from head-to-toe, as if the mountains rewarded fashion choices. Trevor wore a brand-new hiking jacket with the tags still attached.

Jamie sighed internally.

Davis muttered beside him, "Are they serious?"

"Unfortunately," he replied.

The brothers turned as Jamie and Davis walked up. Anthony slapped Jamie on the back hard enough to register on the Richter scale.

"Calloway!" Anthony bellowed. "Thought you'd ditched us."

"Would've," Jamie deadpanned, "but I need your money."

Trevor snorted. "Ha! Good one."

Anthony's grin faltered as he noticed Davis. "And this is?"

"Davis," Jamie said. "She's shadowing me for the year."

"Shadowing?" Trevor asked. "Like an apprentice?"

Jamie opened his mouth to give a vague, non-lawyer-invoking explanation.

"She's vegan," Davis announced flatly, crossing her arms. "The last thing I would do is apprentice to a hunter."

The brothers stared at her the way men often stare at a pothole they should drive around.

Trevor whispered loudly, "Can vegans go camping?"

"Yes," she said, expression sweetly acidic. "We're allowed outdoors. Shocking, I know."

Jamie pinched the bridge of his nose. Ten days in, he'd learned one thing: Davis in a mood was a contact sport.

Anthony cleared his throat. "So, you're, uh, comfortable being around hunters?"

"No," she said. "But here we are."

Trevor looked at Jamie. "This gonna be a problem?"

"No," Jamie said quickly. "She understands the rules."

Davis made a noise that landed somewhere between a scoff and a threat.

Jamie grabbed his pack and motioned them forward. "Let's get moving. We've got a five-hour hike up the ridge, and we want to make it before nightfall."

The brothers trudged forward.

Davis lingered beside him.

"You okay?" he asked quietly.

"Just peachy," she muttered. "I get to spend the day watching people murder an animal with curly horns. What a treat."

"Bighorn sheep," he corrected. "And those horns keep them from being defenseless."

She glared. "They're sheep."

"Yes."

"With legs the width of pretzel sticks."

"They're actually incredibly agile and—"

"Jamie," she hissed, "they can't punch anybody."

He sighed. This was going to be a long day.

The ascent started easy. The trail wound through tall pines, sunlight filtering through in warm patches. Birds chirped overhead; small animals darted through brush.

Trevor and Anthony marched loudly. Too loudly. Jamie winced every time they cracked a branch or scraped their boots over rocks. Bighorn sheep weren't delicate creatures, but they weren't stupid either.

Davis stayed close to Jamie, her breaths even, her steps sure. She wasn't slowing them down. That surprised him.

What didn't surprise him was her commentary.

"So," she said, "how exactly does one hunt a sheep? Do you creep up behind it? Distract it with snacks? Whisper betrayal into its fluffy ear?"

"Davis."

"Oh wait," she said, "are you going to wrestle it? Do people wrestle sheep?"

"No."

"They should. At least it would be more fair."

He stopped walking. "Fair? You want me to wrestle a bighorn sheep?"

"Yes."

"You want me to square up with a one-hundred-eighty-pound muscular animal with horns capable of cracking human ribs?"

"Yes," she repeated brightly.

He stared at her. "You're insane."

She lifted her chin defiantly. "No, I'm ethical."

"You're stubborn."

"And you're insensitive."

They glared at each other for a long beat.

Anthony shouted from ahead, "Hey! Lovebirds! You coming?"

Jamie shut his eyes. Great.

Davis looked like she wanted to throw herself off the mountain.

"We're not—!" she started, but Jamie gently put a hand on her pink backpack strap.

"Let it go," he murmured. "They're idiots."

She grumbled but kept walking.

As they climbed, the trees thinned, and the terrain shifted into rocky slopes. The air grew cooler.

Jamie stopped, held up a fist, the universal signal for silence.

The brothers froze.

Davis froze a heartbeat later.

Jamie crouched and pointed across the ravine.

Three bighorn sheep grazed on a distant ledge. They were majestic, sturdy creatures built for the impossible angles of mountain living. Their curved horns caught the sunlight.

Beautiful animals, even Jamie could admit that.

And Davis?

"Oh no," she whispered, eyes wide with horror. "Absolutely not."

Trevor raised his rifle slightly.

Davis stepped in front of him like a furious woodland guardian. "Put that down!"

Trevor jumped back. "Jesus, call off your wife, Calloway!"

"She is not my," Jamie stopped himself. "Davis, move."

"No," she said fiercely. "They're eating grass. Grass. They're living their little sheep lives."

Jamie stepped close, lowering his voice. "We're not shooting anything from here. It's too far. We're just observing."

"Observing who?" she whispered. "The sheep or the men with guns?"

He exhaled slowly. "Davis."

"What?"

"This is the job."

"It's murder."

"It's regulated wildlife management."

She turned her face toward him, outraged. "You can't manage something by killing it."

"That's literally how it works."

"It shouldn't be!"

Her eyes were bright in a real, raw way he hadn't seen from her before.

Jamie swallowed.

The brothers whispered between themselves.

Anthony: "This is awkward."

Trevor: "Dude, she's terrifying."

Jamie ignored them.

"Look," he said softly, "I'm not asking you to be okay with it. I'm asking you to stay close and trust me."

She breathed sharply through her nose. "I can stay close. But trusting you?" she murmured, "that's the hard part."

He knew what she meant. He also knew she wasn't wrong.

"Just keep an open mind," he said, softer still.

She hesitated longer than he expected.

Finally: "I'll watch. But I won't pretend I like it."

"That's all I ask."

She nodded once.

Then, unexpectedly, she took half a step closer. She was close enough that her shoulder brushed his arm.

Trevor whispered loudly, "Ohhhkay, tension."

Anthony elbowed him. "Dude, shut up."

Davis shot them both a murderous look.

Jamie almost smiled.

Almost.

Then he turned back to the trail and prepared for the long, unpredictable day ahead.

Today wasn't just a hunt.

It was Davis's first real test on his way of life.

Chapter Nine

DAVIS

The sheep vanished almost as soon as Davis blinked.

One moment they were there with majestic, curved horns glinting in the sun, and the next, they'd darted behind a cluster of boulders as if they sensed hunters breathing down their woolly necks.

Good for them, she thought. Run, sheep. Run like your little grass-eating lives depend on it because it does. She literally felt sick at the thought of their deaths.

Jamie crouched to study tracks near the ridge, all quiet focus and outdoorsy competence. The brothers hovered nearby, whispering about angles and distance and shot placement as though it were father-son bonding at a shooting range.

Davis wanted to scream.

Instead, she breathed through her nose and followed Jamie along a narrow ledge carved into the mountainside. Her palms were sweaty, which she refused to admit. The incline was steeper now, the air thinner, the rocks sharper, and the drop-off beside her so dramatic it felt personal.

"Watch your footing," Jamie said gently as she stepped over a jutting rock.

"I'm fine," she said.

She was not fine.

She planted her next step, and the gravel beneath her boot shifted. Fast. Too fast.

Her stomach lurched. The world tilted.

Then nothing but air beneath her foot and she slipped. A sharp cry tore out of her before she could stop it. She reached for anything. Rock, dirt, divine assistance, but gravity didn't care.

Jamie did.

His arm wrapped around her waist with startling force. Another caught her forearm. She crashed into his chest, her boot skidding helplessly over the ledge until he hauled her back against solid ground.

Her heart thundered. Her breath came fast. His grip was iron-tight, anchoring her to his body like she weighed nothing at all.

"Easy," he murmured. "I've got you."

She realized two things immediately: One, he had, in fact, saved her life. Two, she was pressed entirely against him, chest to chest, thigh to thigh, breath mingling.

Her brain short-circuited.

"I'm fine," she managed, though it sounded unconvincing even to her.

He didn't release her right away. "You're shaking."

"I just slipped."

"You almost fell off a mountain."

"Yes, well, a minor detail."

His mouth twitched. Adrenaline-laced laughter pushed at her ribs. Oh no. She would not laugh. Not while she was still wrapped around him like a terrified koala.

He finally loosened his hold but didn't step fully back. "Next time," he said, "stay closer."

"So you can fall first?"

"So I can catch you before you do something stupid."

"I didn't do something stupid," she snapped.

He tilted his head. "You always get snippy after I save you?"

She opened her mouth.

Closed it.

Opened it again.

"I'm not snippy. I'm grateful."

"Could've fooled me."

She glared at him until he smiled, that slow, infuriating smile warm enough to melt snowcaps.

The brothers, of course, had watched the entire moment.

Anthony cupped his hands around his mouth. "Nice catch, Calloway! Didn't know this trip came with romance."

Trevor laughed like a man who'd never had a real date. "Man, she jumped right into your arms."

Davis bristled. "I slipped."

"Sure, honey," Trevor said, winking. "If you say so."

Jamie stepped forward so fast the brothers immediately shut up.

His voice held an edge. "Knock it off."

Anthony lifted his hands in surrender. "Hey, we're kidding."

Trevor added, "Yeah, lighten up."

"No," Jamie said, his jaw tightening. "Not about her."

Heat shot to Davis's cheeks.

Not anger, but shock.

Jamie realized she was listening and looked away quickly, pretending to adjust his pack. But she saw it. The protective flash. The unspoken warning.

The rest of the climb was quieter.

They reached a flat stretch beneath the ridge late in the afternoon. It held just enough space for tents and a fire ring. The sun dipped behind the peaks, bathing the landscape in orange-pink light. It was enough sun to see by as they set up camp.

Davis stared at the pile of nylon, poles, and stakes on the ground like it was a complicated alien organism that had fallen out of the sky. The packaging said the tent was "intuitive."

Intuitive for *who*?

Certainly not for someone who'd spent her formative years learning plant-based nutrition instead of wilderness survival.

Across the small clearing, Jamie was already halfway done pitching his own tent in a maddeningly competent fashion. His movements were practiced as if the tent simply knew better than to argue with him.

She glared at her own heap again.

"Okay," she muttered. "I've read the instructions. I've watched the videos. I've got this."

She absolutely did not have this.

The first pole bent in a warped way. The second popped apart like a slinky with abandonment issues. When she tried to clip two pieces of fabric together, the tent collapsed into a sad puddle around her ankles.

Jamie finally looked over, and the bastard had the audacity to smirk.

"You planning to sleep inside that?" he asked.

She planted her hands on her hips. "Yes."

"In its current state?"

"It's in progress."

"It looks dead."

She sucked in a calming breath. "You could offer to help."

"No," he said instantly.

Her jaw dropped. "No?"

"Nope." He snapped a stake into the ground with effortless precision. "You're supposed to learn the way of the hunter. That includes setting up your own shelter."

"I'm learning. I'm learning that tents hate me."

"That's not a tent," he said. "That's a fabric obituary."

She pointed a tent pole at him like a weapon. "Jamie Calloway, if you don't help me, I swear I will—" She didn't finish the statement but stomping her foot had to make a point.

"What?" he asked, amused. "Make me eat tofu?"

"You're already eating tofu."

"Then what's the threat?"

She opened her mouth.

Closed it.

And considered clubbing him with the pole.

Instead, she stomped back to her tent pieces and tried again. She managed to raise the frame for a glorious two seconds before the structure leaned like it'd lost all hope in life and collapsed on top of her.

Jamie chuckled.

Chuckled.

"Are you enjoying this?" she demanded from under a mess of canvas.

"A little."

"You're cruel."

"You're dramatic."

She extricated herself from the tent, hair full of static electricity, pride hanging on by a thread. "You're supposed to be my guide."

"I am." He hooked his thumb toward the half-built tent beside him. "Guiding by example."

"I hate you."

"You say that a lot."

"Because it's often true."

"And yet," he said, leaning against a tree, "you still want my help."

"Only because I'm a human being who deserves a functional shelter!"

Jamie crossed his arms, observing her like a scientist studying a new species.

Finally, after watching her struggle for a solid three additional minutes in which the tent took on six different shapes, none of them inhabitable, he sighed and pushed off the tree.

He walked over and crouched down beside her.

"I'm not doing it for you," he said.

She scowled. "Then for who?"

"For both of us," he said. "If you sleep in a collapsed heap of nylon, you're going to be grumpy tomorrow, and I'm not dealing with that."

Her irritation wavered. "That is almost considerate."

"Don't read too much into it." But his voice was softer now.

And his large hands moved through the tangled poles and fabric with practiced ease. He didn't take over completely; instead, he guided her movements.

"Put that one through the sleeve."

"No, not that sleeve, the other side."

"Tighten that clip."

"Good. Now pull this way."

Their hands brushed just enough to make something warm flicker low in her stomach. Within five minutes, the tent stood upright. It was straight, taut, and perfect.

She stared at it, wide-eyed. "Oh. My God. It looks like a tent."

"It *is* a tent," he said.

"You helped."

"I supervised."

"You're still an ass."

"Probably."

She crossed her arms. "Thank you."

He looked at her for one suspended moment and his expression softened.

"Anytime," he said quietly. Then he cleared his throat, stepped back, and the moment dissolved.

Later, she'd realize she wasn't the only one fighting something that day.

But right then, she only knew one thing: For the first time since arriving in the wilderness, she felt safe.

Jamie started setting up the fire. Davis helped, despite the brothers murmuring behind them about "city vegans" and "delicate stomachs."

Trevor poked at the fire pit. "Hope you brought your own food, sweetheart. We didn't pack any quinoa."

Davis shot him a look. "I brought food. You don't need to worry about me."

Anthony smirked. "Did you bring anything edible?"

"More than you did," she snapped.

Before either man could respond, Jamie stepped between them with his strong presence that made the brothers immediately lose a few inches of confidence.

"She eats fine," he said. "She carries her weight. And she's been more graceful on this mountain than either of you two."

Trevor bristled. "What's that supposed to mean? She nearly fell off."

"It means," Jamie said, dropping a handful of tinder into the ring, "you two sound like idiots."

Silence.

Trevor opened his mouth. Jamie raised a single eyebrow. Trevor shut it.

Anthony muttered, "Damn, man."

Davis bit back a smile. She didn't want them to see how much that meant. But inside, her chest tightened in an odd way.

When the fire finally crackled to life, the brothers wandered off to examine the landscape and pretend they knew what they were doing.

Davis and Jamie sat on opposite logs, the firelight dancing across his face, softening his features into something almost boyish.

"Thanks," she said quietly.

"For what?" he asked, prodding a log.

"For sticking up for me."

He shrugged one shoulder. "They were being jerks."

"That doesn't always stop people and besides, they are paying you for a good time. I mean, not a good time like that but the hunting kind of good time."

He looked at her from across the fire.

"Thank you for clarifying good time, I'm glad I hadn't taken it the wrong way." His expression changed and she would swear she saw hurt in his eyes. "I'm not 'people,' Davis."

A tiny shiver ran through her. It was annoyingly pleasant. "No," she admitted softly. "You're not."

He tossed another stick into the flames. "You did good today."

She snorted. "I slipped off a cliff."

"You handled everything else well."

He leaned forward slightly. "And you trusted me."

She looked away from the fire. Away from him. The trust part hit harder than she expected.

"I was scared."

"Everyone gets scared."

"You don't."

He laughed quietly. "You think I don't get scared?"

"You seem like the type who fights fear with arrogance."

"That is not entirely inaccurate," he said with a grin.

She smiled back before she could stop herself.

The fire popped. Sparks rose into the dusk.

For a long moment, neither of them spoke.

It wasn't silence.

It was something else.

This was the kind of quiet where two people breathe in sync without meaning to.

Finally, he said, "Tomorrow'll be tougher. More climbing. More tracking."

She nodded. "I'll manage."

"I know you will."

Her heart fluttered.

He leaned forward, elbows on his knees. "Davis?"

"Yes?" she whispered.

"Just stay close."

Her pulse skipped. "I will."

A branch snapped somewhere behind them. The brothers muttered something about dinner. The moment broke but only just.

Davis settled back, pulling her jacket tighter around her.

Tomorrow would be hard. Terrifying, even.

But tonight?

She wasn't afraid. Not with him sitting opposite her, watching the fire, shoulders relaxed for the first time all day.

Not with him on her side.

Not with something between them she wasn't ready to name.

She just knew it was there.

And growing.

Chapter Ten

JAMIE

Anthony and Trevor retired to their tent. Within ten minutes, both men were snoring. Davis didn't look tired; she looked energized.

"Do you think about the animals you kill?" she asked softly.

"Think about them how?" he asked.

"They have lives. They help each other and have sheep they care about."

"You're giving them too much credit," he said. "Do you know that vegans are more hated than terrorists?"

"We're activists. Of course we're hated. You didn't answer my question."

Jamie poked at the fire with a stick that didn't deserve the abuse. Sparks flared upward, casting brief gold across Davis's face. She looked fierce, stubborn, and, unfortunately for his sanity, incredibly beautiful in that way people looked when they truly believed in something.

He wasn't used to that. Passion pointed in the opposite direction of his own.

"Do I think about them?" he repeated, buying time, because her eyes were doing the thing where they stripped the bullshit off a man and expected something real underneath.

She waited.

He genuinely cared for the forest and its wildlife, which was why the kill was always a serious transaction. Ethically, he viewed hunting not as a sport, but as a crucial, if brutal, act of conservation. It was a harsh but necessary tool for balancing an ecosystem that human intrusion had permanently skewed. But beyond the science, there was a deeper, primal drive. In a world drowned in glowing screens and soft, digital noise, he felt men were losing their connection to the earth, desperately needing a difficult, honest challenge to reconnect with the raw reality of being alive.

Damn it.

"Yeah," he finally said. "Of course I think about them. I'm not a robot."

"Could've fooled me," she murmured.

He ignored that. Mostly.

He leaned forward, elbows on his knees. "You want the truth?"

"I asked for it."

"The truth is, I respect them."

She blinked, surprise softening her mouth for half a second. "You respect the animals you kill?"

"I respect the way they live," he said. "The way they fight. The way they survive storms and winters and predators without asking anyone's permission. They're strong. They're built for this world."

Her brows drew together. "And so you shoot them."

He flinched, just barely. "Yeah," he admitted. "And you hate that."

"I do," she whispered. Not ashamed. Not apologetic. Just honest.

He dragged a hand through his hair. "I don't expect you to see it my way. Hell, most people don't. But for what it's worth, I take it seriously. Every damn time. It isn't just a notch on a belt."

Davis stared at the fire with her jaw tight. "Sometimes I wish you were an asshole about it."

"I can be an asshole about plenty of other things."

"That's true."

He nudged her boot with his. "You okay?"

"No."

"Fair."

He watched her for a long beat. The firelight made her look softer, rounder at the edges, like she wasn't trying to hold up so much of her own anger alone.

He didn't like hurting her. It twisted something in his chest he didn't have a name for.

"Davis."

She didn't look at him. "Hm?"

"You were wrong earlier."

That got her attention. She lifted her gaze, wary. "About what?"

"You said the sheep care about each other."

"And they do."

Jamie shook his head slowly. "Not the way you mean. Not the way you want them to."

She frowned. "You don't know that."

"Yes, I do. Animals don't think like us. They don't mourn the same. They don't sit around thinking about ethics or choices or what their purpose is on the planet. They don't feel guilt. Or shame. They're clean that way."

She swallowed. "And people aren't."

"People are messy," he said. "People overthink everything."

"People like me?" she asked.

"People like you," he said, his tone gentler than he intended, "think so hard about what's right that they can't see anyone else's version of it."

Her breath hitched a little. "You're calling me close-minded?"

"No." He reached out and plucked a pine needle off her sleeve. "I'm calling you someone who cares too much to see gray areas. And I get that. I do."

She stared at him. Really stared. The kind of look that made a man want to rearrange his life so she'd never stop doing it.

But then she whispered, "What if I don't want gray areas?"

His chest tightened. "Too bad. The world's full of them."

She dropped her gaze to the fire. "I hate that."

"I know."

The silence that stretched between them was oddly comforting. The fire crackled and sighed. A breeze tugged strands of hair loose from her braid.

He didn't plan on speaking again.

But he did.

"I meant what I said earlier."

She glanced up. "Which part?"

"That I'm not 'people.'" He smirked faintly. "Not the way you meant it."

She arched one eyebrow. "Oh? And what are you then?"

He leaned back slightly, pretending like the answer wasn't the most dangerous truth he'd spoken in a while.

"I don't judge you for who you are," he murmured. "Even when who you are annoys the hell out of me."

Her lips parted. Not in offense. In something else.

"Jamie," she whispered.

He held her gaze, the fire popping loud between them. "Yeah?"

She opened her mouth.

But didn't answer.

Instead, she looked away quickly, pulling her knees closer to her chest as though bracing herself.

The moment shifted. Faded. Turned into something quieter, but no less heavy.

Jamie swallowed hard, unsure if he was relieved or disappointed.

Probably both.

He grabbed a log and tossed it onto the fire. "We should sleep soon. Tomorrow's going to be rough."

She nodded but didn't get up.

He didn't either.

"Vegans care about animals," she said softly. "Animals are sentient beings who have feelings. Yes, they mourn. Until you see a calf pulled from its mother so she can provide milk to humans and not her baby, you won't understand. That mother mourns the loss of her baby. I fight because the cow doesn't have a choice in its life and it doesn't deserve to have its baby pulled away."

She went quiet after that. They sat at the fire longer than they needed to, staring at the flames, pretending they weren't sitting in the middle of one.

Chapter Eleven

DAVIS

She woke with the unmistakable sense that someone was breathing far too close to her face.

Davis opened one eye cautiously.

Jamie.

Jamie Calloway was crouched at the entrance of her tent like some smug, shirtless wilderness gargoyle.

"Morning," he whispered, way too loud for a whisper.

She yelped, grabbed her mini-pillow, and instinctively launched it at his face.

He caught it midair; because of course he did. Where was a fifteen-pound package of tofu when you needed one?

"What is wrong with you?" she hissed. No, she wouldn't comment on the fact his nipples were tightly puckered from the cold or that each rippling chest muscle looked good enough to lick.

"Rise and shine," he said cheerfully. "It's 4:58."

She glared. "Two minutes early? Are you serious?"

"Always." He tossed the pillow back at her. "Gear up. We've got climbing today."

She flopped backward onto her thin camping pad. "I hope a bird poops on your head."

He smirked. "Wouldn't be the first time. Though usually they're not vegan."

"Birds aren't vegan," she muttered.

"Well," he said, stretching like a smug jungle cat, "they're not carnivores either. They're middle-of-the-road. Like you, actually—"

She sat up so fast his words died in his throat.

"Like me?"

"Emotionally," he added quickly. "Emotionally middle-of-the-road."

"That isn't better."

He grinned.

She scowled.

Mother Nature, in all her cruelty, decided at that exact moment to paint him in sunrise light as gold slanted across his jaw, his bare shoulders, and his arms.

His shirtless, glistening-from-the-morning-air arms.

Terrific.

He noticed the glance, of course he did. Jamie noticed everything.

"Like what you see?" he asked.

"No," she said immediately.

He lifted a brow. "You said no too fast."

"I said it exactly fast enough."

"You can say yes," he teased. "I don't charge extra for early-morning appreciation."

She grabbed her boot and threw it at him.

He dodged easily, laughing. "Hurry up. I need to check the ridge before the brothers wake up."

"Do they ever wake up?" she muttered. "Or are they born complaining?"

Jamie's lips twitched. "You're not wrong."

He disappeared from the tent flap, leaving her to dress and mutter threats that would make a mountain lion blush.

Forty minutes later, Davis was fully caffeinated. Sane people drank tea; insane people wore no shirts before 5 a.m. in the mountains.

The brothers emerged from their tent looking like hungover walruses.

Anthony groaned. "Dude, why is it cold?"

"Because it's morning," Jamie said, deadpan.

Trevor shivered dramatically. "Feels like," he stopped before muttering, "weather."

Davis blinked slowly. "You two are going to hunt something today?"

Anthony puffed up. "We're outdoorsmen."

"You tripped on a pinecone last night."

"It was dark!"

"It was not," she said flatly. "The fire was blazing like a small sun."

Jamie snorted.

Trevor grumbled something about hostile vegans.

Jamie shot him a look, and blessed silence returned.

Davis went through her backpack and pulled out a loaf of her famous bread, along with a tub of homemade vegan butter. She toasted the bread in a small pan that also came from her backpack.

She saw the looks Jamie cast at her bread, but she didn't offer him any. The men ate something from Jamie's pack that looked cold and unappetizing. She hoped it was.

After breakfast and a quick gear check, Jamie nodded toward the ridge. "Let's move."

They headed up the slope, the world around them cool in the morning light. Birds called in the distance. Pine needles crunched underfoot.

Every step upward made Davis's heart pound. It wasn't fear. It pounded from anger. From dread. From everything tangled up inside her that she wasn't ready to unravel.

Jamie walked beside her, annoyingly calm. "You're breathing weird," he said.

"I'm climbing," she snapped.

"You're muttering, too."

"I always mutter."

"What are you muttering about now?"

"You."

"Of course."

She shoved past him, because if she didn't, she'd accidentally like him today, and that was unacceptable on a killing day.

They climbed higher, the terrain rough beneath their boots. Davis was careful. Extra careful. Yesterday's slip had seared itself into her memory like a flashing neon sign reading *you almost died, idiot.*

But the view.

God.

The mountains rolled out before them in endless blue-gray waves, sunlight catching the far-off peaks like sunshine on steel. This was true nature in all its glory. It should be allowed to remain this way. Forever.

"Wow," she breathed before she could stop herself.

Jamie glanced sideways. "Yeah," he said softly. "Worth the climb."

She hated that he had that gentle tone. Ugh. He was an animal killer, and she had to remember that.

They continued up another steep incline, and that's when she felt it, a shift. A tremor of rock beneath her feet.

"Jamie."

He heard it too. His hand shot out, gripping her backpack strap just as the gravel under her right foot gave way. She pitched forward with a small cry.

He hauled her back, until the rumble settled.

Breathing hard, she whispered, "That wasn't me being clumsy."

"No," he said. "That was the mountain being an asshole."

She nodded shakily. "I prefer blaming the mountain."

"Good. Stick with that."

He didn't let go until her legs steadied.

Behind them, Trevor called, "You two good? Need a moment? Want us to look away?"

Jamie turned with a look that could have ended bloodlines. Trevor pretended very hard to adjust his shoelace.

They continued upward in a tense silence.

Then they saw it.

A lone bighorn sheep stood on a small rocky shelf overlooking a narrow ravine. Alone. No herd. No protection. Just one quiet creature with soft eyes and a body built for cliffs and sky.

Davis stopped dead.

"Oh," she whispered.

It lifted its head, ears flicking, watching them with curiosity, not fear. It was beautiful. Perfect. Alive.

"Jamie," she murmured, voice breaking. "Please. They don't need to—"

But she wasn't given the chance to finish.

A crack split the morning air.

A gunshot.

The sheep jerked sideways, legs collapsing beneath it. It fell hard, sliding down the slanted rock until it hit a narrow ledge and stilled.

A raw scream tore out from Davis.

"No!"

Jamie spun toward the brothers. "What the hell? I didn't give the signal!"

Anthony shrugged, lowering his rifle. "It was a clean shot."

Trevor grinned. "Got it on the first try."

"You shot it?" Davis yelled, storming toward them. "It was just standing there! It wasn't." She took a breath before finishing, "It wasn't even doing anything!"

"It's an animal," Anthony said defensively. "That's what we're here for."

"It was alive," she shouted. "You killed it like it was nothing!"

Jamie grabbed her arm. Not harshly, but firmly, to keep her from charging directly at Anthony. "Davis, hey, stop."

She yanked her arm free, tears stinging her eyes. "No! Don't ask me to stop! You told me this wasn't just killing. You told me you respected them!"

"I do," Jamie said quietly. His expression wasn't cold. It was hard. "And that's why I'm pissed."

Trevor scoffed. "It's a sheep, man."

Jamie turned so slowly that Trevor actually took a step back.

"You ever fire again without my word," Jamie said, his voice dangerous, "and you're done. I'll drag you off this mountain by your overpriced jacket."

Anthony rolled his eyes. "We got the kill. Why are you throwing a fit?"

"Because you didn't wait," Jamie snapped. "Because you didn't listen. Because you ignored every safety rule."

Davis couldn't breathe.

Her chest felt too tight. Her throat too thick.

The sheep's still body lay far below them. She couldn't stop staring.

She whispered, "It didn't even run."

Jamie looked at her then. Really looked. Something in his face cracked. Just slightly.

"Davis, don't go down there," he said softly.

She wiped her eyes angrily. "I wasn't planning to."

"We have to move," he said gently. "We'll circle down the long way. Safely."

She nodded, but didn't feel her head move.

The world felt a little dimmer. A little colder. A little crueler.

Jamie stepped closer, voice low. "Hey."

She didn't lift her gaze.

"Davis."

He waited until she met his eyes.

"I'm right here," he said.

And despite everything. Despite the pain, the anger, the heartbreak of it, she believed him.

Even if she hated that she did.

Chapter Twelve

DAVIS

The descent to the ledge felt like wading through wet cement. Every step she took was weighted with dread. The brothers hung back with forced nonchalance, their weapons slung carelessly over their shoulders. Davis didn't look at them. Couldn't. If she did, she couldn't be held responsible for the number of ways she'd consider violently rearranging their kneecaps.

Jamie kept her in front of him, his voice steady whenever the trail narrowed.

"Step left. Careful. Rock's loose here."

She obeyed without speaking. She wasn't sure she could speak. Breathing was hard enough.

When they finally reached the narrow ledge where the sheep had fallen, Davis stopped.

It lay on its side, legs tucked awkwardly, blood matting its wool. Its eyes were partially open; dark, glassy, and unseeing.

Something broke inside her chest.

Slowly, she sank to her knees beside it.

"Oh," she whispered, her voice trembling. "Oh God."

Jamie crouched beside her but didn't touch her. Didn't try to move her. Just stayed close enough that she could feel his presence.

She reached out with shaking fingers, then hesitated.

"Can I?" she whispered.

"Yeah," he said quietly. "You can."

Her hand brushed the wool. It was softer than she expected. Still warm.

Her throat closed.

"It was just standing here," she choked. "Existing. Breathing. Looking at us. And now it's—"

Her voice broke entirely.

Jamie exhaled, the sound rough at the edges. "I know."

"No," she snapped, tears hot on her cheeks. "You don't know."

He didn't argue.

Didn't deflect.

Didn't try to use logic or biology or predator-prey cycles to talk her out of it.

He just stayed quiet.

The grief came in waves. It was overwhelming, irrational, and yet painfully real. She pressed a hand over her mouth to stop the sob that forced its way out anyway.

Jamie's hand landed gently on her back.

She didn't shrug him off.

She couldn't.

He said nothing, and somehow that made her cry harder.

"It didn't hurt long," he murmured eventually. "The shot was clean."

"Don't," she whispered fiercely. "Don't make it sound better. It's dead."

"I'm not trying to make it better," he said. "I'm telling you the truth. It matters."

"To you," she choked. "Not to me."

He hesitated. "It matters to me that it would matter to you."

She turned slowly, looking at him through tears. His expression was carved with frustration at the brothers, at the situation, maybe even at himself, but underneath that was something softer, something she didn't know what to do with.

"I hate this," she whispered.

"I know."

"I hate them."

"I know."

"I hate you too."

He nodded. "You're allowed."

She wiped her face with the heel of her hand. "Why didn't you stop them?"

His jaw tightened. "Because I wasn't expecting them to ignore every instruction I gave. Because they're reckless idiots. Because I was watching you and not them."

Her breath caught. "Watching me?"

He looked away, but not fast enough.

"Yes," he said quietly. "You."

She didn't know what to do with that. Not now.

"Can we...?" She swallowed hard. "Can we do something for it? I don't know what. I just, I can't leave it like this."

Jamie nodded. "Yeah. We can." He turned to the brothers. "The two of you take a hike. You can get your pictures in a bit."

They left, and Jamie stood and walked a few feet to gather a small handful of long branches. He brought them back and arranged them gently around the sheep's body, forming a kind of natural barrier. Not a burial. Not a monument. But a marker.

Respect.

She helped; her fingers numb. When they finished, Jamie stepped back and gave her space.

Davis rested her hand once more on the sheep's side. "I'm sorry," she whispered.

Jamie bowed his head slightly, the way a person might at a graveside.

After a moment, he spoke. "Davis, you need to know something. Hunters, good ones, they don't take more than the land can handle. The tag system keeps balance. The herds stay healthy. It's not mindless."

"Then why does it feel like it is?" she whispered.

"Because you feel everything," he said softly. "That's your strength. And your weakness."

She closed her eyes. A tear slid down.

Jamie continued, keeping his voice low. "You care about life. In a big, loud, overwhelming way. And sometimes that makes the world look crueler than it is." He paused. "But sometimes it also makes the world better than it is."

Her eyes snapped open. His unguarded gaze remained on her.

It stole her breath.

But she couldn't deal with that. Not here, not with blood on the rock and a creature lying still at her knees.

So she pushed herself to her feet.

Jamie rose with her.

"We need to get back to camp," he said. "Before they do something else stupid."

She nodded. But before they turned away, she whispered one last time to the little life extinguished on the mountainside: "You deserved better."

Jamie didn't touch her, but he walked close enough that their arms brushed.

The brothers had stayed back. When Jamie saw them, he waved them to the dead sheep for their trophy pictures.

His presence didn't steady her. But it kept her from falling apart again.

And for now, that was enough.

Chapter Thirteen

DAVIS

She stayed at the camp for thirty minutes before deciding to take a short walk to steady her nerves. When Davis walked back into camp, she felt like a wrung-out sponge someone had used to wipe up feelings. Too many feelings. Grief, anger, guilt, nausea, and an inconvenient dash of "Jamie has a chest I could write poetry about," which seemed deeply inappropriate given the circumstances.

The brothers sat near the fire pit eating jerky like nothing had happened.

Jerky.

Could she throw them off the mountain and get away with it? Or at least hide their boots so they'd have to descend barefoot and grow a personality.

Jamie walked close and muttered under his breath, "Stay with me."

"You don't own me," she hissed.

"Didn't say I did. I'm just preventing a homicide."

"A justified homicide."

"A lot of paperwork."

He stepped forward, shoulders tense. "Nobody moves," he warned the brothers.

Trevor, mid-chew, froze like a cow in headlights. "What? We're not doing anything."

"Exactly," Davis snapped. "You're not doing anything. Like thinking!"

Anthony sighed dramatically. "Here we go."

"Oh, you want a show?" she asked sweetly. "I can give you a show."

Jamie put a hand over her mouth.

Which was a mistake.

A huge mistake.

Because she tasted the faint salt and pine from his palm, and her brain short-circuited so hard she forgot what anger even was.

She swatted his hand away as reality rebooted. "Don't touch me!"

"You were about to lunge," Jamie said calmly. "I'm protecting everyone's life, including yours."

"Tackle them yourself," she snapped.

"Tempting," he murmured.

Anthony and Trevor looked very suddenly interested in the ground.

Jamie turned to them. "Pack your gear. We're heading back early."

"What?" Trevor yelped. "But we didn't get the other—"

"Say one more word," Jamie said, "and you can roll down the mountain instead of walk."

Trevor's mouth shut so fast it made an audible click.

Davis, meanwhile, was still vibrating with leftover emotions. Her body felt like she was one sip of tea away from sobbing again, or screaming, or both.

She needed distance.

Oxygen.

Space.

She stalked toward her tent, but Jamie followed.

"You need to eat," he said.

"I need to be alone."

"You need to eat."

"I need to bury my emotions under a sleeping bag!"

He hesitated. "Okay, that part I understand."

She turned and glared at him. "Jamie, please. Just give me five minutes."

He nodded. "Five. But if you're not back by then, I'm dragging you out and making you eat a granola bar."

She sneered. "Your granola bars have beef fat in them."

He winced. "Okay, I'll find the vegan ones."

"Please don't."

"Too late," he said, already rummaging in his pack.

"Oh my God," she groaned.

She ducked inside her tent.

Five minutes later. Exactly five minutes later, Jamie unzipped the tent flap without preamble.

"Your time's up. Eat this."

She didn't look. "If that's beef jerky, I'll feed it to a squirrel and let it judge your soul."

"It's dried mango."

She perked up slightly. "Really?"

"Yes. It's obnoxiously sweet, and I hate it."

She looked at the bag cautiously.

Jamie held out the bag of mango like an offering to a grumpy mountain goddess.

"You bought this?" she asked.

"No," he said. "My sister sent it to me as a joke when she found out about the contents of the will. Said it might 'open my mind.' It didn't."

She took the bag. "Thank you. I think I like your sister."

"You're welcome. You would like all of them."

"All. How many?"

"Five."

"You're kidding?"

"No and I'm the youngest."

"That explains so much." She ate a piece. And another. And then the entire bag, because trauma hunger was real.

Jamie sat down beside her tent opening, arms resting on his knees. "I thought you didn't like processed food."

"I like it when my soul is in crisis."

"Should I pack more soul-crisis snacks?"

She blinked. "Are you teasing me gently?"

He shrugged. "Sometimes I try variety."

"Try sarcasm less often."

"No."

She snorted, a tiny puff of laughter escaping before she could stop it.

Jamie saw.

His grin softened and became less cocky, more warm.

"You okay now?" he asked.

"No."

"Okay," he said. "Want me to sit here and be quiet with you?"

She hesitated.

Then nodded.

He sat.

She leaned back against her pack.

They didn't speak.

They didn't need to.

For several minutes, only the wind moved through the trees, rustling leaves like someone whispering secrets they weren't ready to hear.

Finally, he cleared his throat. "So," he said dryly, "I have an important logistical question."

She frowned. "What?"

"In the event of my death, which could easily happen given your murderous energy, would you at least pretend to mourn?"

She stared at him.

Then whispered, "Depends."

"On what?"

"Will you haunt me?"

He blinked. "What?"

"If you die first," she said, "you'll absolutely haunt me out of spite."

He considered. "Yeah. Probably."

"Then no," she said primly. "I won't mourn you. I'll sage the house."

He laughed.

She smiled.

And just like that, something inside her loosened.

Not healed. Not fixed.

Just lighter.

The grief was still there along with the anger.

But so was he.

Stupid, shirtless, sarcastic, emotionally confusing Jamie.

Chapter Fourteen

DAVIS

The estate felt different when they returned. Not bigger or smaller. Not better or worse. Just quieter.

Like the walls had decided to give her space to breathe, or maybe they sensed she'd had enough emotional whiplash for one hunting trip.

Davis dropped her backpack on the entryway rug and winced when her shoulder protested. Her body ached in new and creative places: hiking muscles, crying muscles, almost-falling-off-a-mountain muscles.

Jamie brushed past her, carrying the heavy gear like he hadn't been dragged through emotional gravel as well.

"Shower," he said over his shoulder. "Go. You smell like trauma."

She blinked. "Did you just tell me to shower?"

"Yes."

"Jamie, I swear—"

"Davis."

He pointed at the staircase.

His tone was soft.

Too soft.

She shut her mouth and trudged upstairs.

Steam curled around her as hot water hit her sore shoulders. She leaned a hand against the tile, eyes closed, letting the heat melt away the ache lodged somewhere between her ribs.

She didn't cry.

She wasn't going to cry anymore today. She was done crying. She had reached the legal limit of tears for the next forty-eight hours.

When she finally stepped out, wrapped in her softest robe with damp hair hanging down her back, she expected the house to feel empty.

But Jamie was in the kitchen.

Barefoot. Hair damp from his own recent shower. Gray T-shirt clinging in ways that should be illegal in several states.

He was standing over the stove.

Cooking.

Davis stopped in the doorway. "Are you making food?"

He startled slightly but covered it quickly. "Don't sound so horrified."

"I am horrified. What are you cooking? Poison?"

His mouth twitched. "It's soup."

Soup.

Jamie Calloway.

Soup.

"This feels suspicious," she said slowly.

"It's just vegetables."

Her eyes narrowed. "What kind of vegetables?"

"The kind you eat."

"That tells me nothing."

He sighed exaggeratedly. "Carrots, potatoes, onions. Relax. No animals were harmed in the making of this soup."

That sentence shouldn't have hit her in the chest.

But it did.

She stepped closer. "Why are you making this?"

He stirred the pot. "Because you like soup." He cleared his throat. "And because the past forty-eight hours have been a lot."

She blinked. "You're comforting me with soup."

"Don't make it weird," he muttered, turning away to ladle some into a bowl.

Her lips parted. "Jamie."

"Sit," he said, sliding the bowl toward her.

So she sat.

He placed the bowl in front of her, then leaned on the opposite side of the island, watching.

Waiting.

She took a cautious spoonful.

Warm. Savory. Simple in a way that felt like an embrace she didn't have to admit she needed.

"It's good," she said quietly.

His shoulders loosened, just a fraction.

"Yeah?"

She nodded. "Yeah."

He rubbed the back of his neck, looking annoyed with himself. "Okay. Good."

She ate another spoonful. "Jamie, why did you really make this?"

He swallowed. "Because you didn't sleep much last night and you've had a very bad day."

Her breath hitched. "Oh."

"And you've, I don't know. Been holding everything inside." He gestured vaguely. "Thought warm food might help."

She looked down.

He hesitated. Then said, "You don't have to be okay yet."

Her eyes stung again. Traitors. She set the spoon down before she dropped it.

"I hate that you know that," she whispered.

He stepped around the counter. Slowly. Giving her space to bolt if she wanted to.

She didn't bolt.

He leaned against the island beside her, close enough she felt the heat of him. "Davis."

She looked up.

His eyes were gentle in a way that made her heart twist.

"You can talk to me. If you want."

"I don't know what to say."

"Then don't. Just sit."

She did.

And he stayed beside her without touching, without crowding her, without trying to fix her.

Just stayed.

The warmth between them grew thicker than the steam rising from her soup.

Finally, she whispered, "I didn't expect this. You don't need to take care of me."

He looked at her like she had said the dumbest thing imaginable. "Of course I did."

Her pulse tripped. "Why?"

His jaw flexed.

He looked away.

Then back.

Because he was Jamie, he didn't say the easy thing. He said the true thing. "Because it's you," he said softly.

She didn't move.

He didn't either.

And the silence between them wasn't painful or tense this time. It was warm, intimate, and entirely new territory for both of them.

She finally took another spoonful of soup, her voice barely above a whisper. "Thank you."

Jamie nodded once, his eyes lingering on her like he was memorizing every inch of her.

"You're welcome," he said. "For the record, you can lean on me. When you need to."

Her heart did something traitorous.

But all she said was, "Maybe."

He smirked. "I'll take 'maybe.'"

She smiled faintly into her bowl.

Breathing didn't hurt quite so much now.

Chapter Fifteen

DAVIS

The greenhouse was the only thing keeping her sane, and considering the emotional roller coaster of inheriting a mansion and a hunter with opinions, sanity was a fragile commodity.

From digging up planter boxes to rewiring irrigation lines that looked like a failed game of Twister, it was the kind of work she loved almost more than cooking. Almost. She'd already ordered new seeds for recipes she wanted to test for her next cookbook. The book wouldn't release until next year, but she needed months to document the grow patterns, troubleshoot sprouting disasters, and determine which vegetable played nicely with others. Spoiler: radishes were tyrants.

Jamie worked too, annoyingly hard. He took her daily honey-do list and demolished it like a man trying to impress a woman he absolutely wasn't trying to impress. He replaced broken greenhouse panes, drove to the hardware store twice in one morning, hauled bags of soil bigger than her hopes and dreams, and did all of it without a single complaint.

He also wandered around the estate fixing whatever problem dared to exist in an old house. There didn't seem to be anything the man couldn't do.

Well, besides consistently forgetting to put on a shirt.

That became a bigger issue when the weather warmed and sweat began to glide down his chest like it had a personal vendetta against her self-control.

Honestly, that one problem should be illegal.

After working the morning in the greenhouse, she met Jamie in the dining room where they were tackling another problem.

The dining room looked different in daylight. Less haunted mansion, more quirky inherited problem. A stack of old boxes sat on the table, each labeled in faded handwriting: *A. Gables, Personal, Estate Plans, Letters, Records.*

Jamie dropped the last box with a grunt. He'd carried them from an unused bedroom closet. "Your great uncle really didn't believe in throwing things away."

Davis brushed dust from her hands. "Maybe he was sentimental."

"Or a hoarder."

She shot him a look. "Can you try not being rude about my dead relative?"

"I can try," he said. "I won't succeed."

She huffed, opening a box marked *Personal*. Photo albums, cracked leather journals, and brittle envelopes. The scent of old paper rose up like a memory from someone else's life.

Jamie leaned over her shoulder. Too closely, too casually, too Jamie.

Their arms brushed.

She pretended not to feel it.

"What's this?" he asked, reaching past her to grab a packet of papers.

His arm fully pressed against hers.

Fully.

She forgot her own name for a second.

"Jamie," she said, voice slightly thinner than intended, "I can reach things myself."

"I know," he said. He didn't move away. "I'm being helpful."

"You're being proximity aggressive."

He smirked. "That's not a thing."

"It is when you do it."

He still didn't move.

Her heart did a weird little stumble.

She flung open the first photo album to distract herself, but that didn't help.

Inside were black-and-white pictures of the estate decades ago, younger people she didn't recognize lounging on the veranda, snapshots of gardens now overgrown.

And one picture of a woman.

Dark hair piled elegantly, striking eyes, a smile like she knew secrets.

"Oh," Davis whispered.

Jamie leaned even closer. "She looks like you. If she had red hair, it would be you."

Her breath caught.

Not because she agreed. She didn't.

She swallowed. "Who is she?"

"Your great-aunt, maybe? Or cousin? I don't know the family tree."

"She's stunning," Davis murmured, running a thumb lightly over the picture.

Jamie's voice dropped. "So are you."

She froze.

The air froze.

Even the dust motes that she should tackle paused midair in solidarity.

Slowly, she turned her head toward him. "What did you say?"

Too late, he seemed to realize he'd said it out loud. His eyes widened a fraction, then narrowed like he was annoyed at his own mouth.

"I said," he cleared his throat, "that the lighting in here is terrible."

She stared. "Jamie."

He looked everywhere except at her. "What?"

"Don't lie. You said—"

He cut her off too quickly. "Look, papers. Legal stuff. Estate mysteries. Focus."

He grabbed a stack of documents, retreating to the opposite end of the table like she was a wild animal and he was covered in barbecue sauce.

Davis watched him for a long moment.

His shoulders were stiff.

His ears were pink.

He was absolutely, unquestionably flustered.

Jamie Calloway.

Flustered.

She slowly picked up another photo, lips curving despite everything. "You can't just say something like that and run away."

"I didn't run," he snapped. "I relocated."

"To the other side of the table."

"It's a very large table," he argued.

She bit back a smile. "Uh-huh."

They worked in tense, charged silence for a few minutes with her occasionally glancing at him and catching him glancing at her first.

Each time, he looked away like a guilty toddler.

Finally, Davis slid a journal toward him. "You can read this one. It looks like notes."

He opened the leather-bound book carefully. "It's his handwriting."

"Your grandfather's or mine?" she asked.

"Your uncle's," he said. "It's dated twenty-five years ago."

She leaned closer, too close, because he smelled divine. And in order to read over his shoulder.

Again, arm contact.

Again, heart betrayal.

Jamie's breath hitched, barely audible.

She wasn't sure he even noticed doing it.

She did.

The journal entry was short: just rambling thoughts about the estate, the greenhouse, a desire to preserve the land rather than "watch it be swallowed by city greed." But at the bottom, a name was scribbled quickly.

Her breath halted.

"Davis," Jamie whispered. "Is that?"

Her name.

Davis Jules.

Written long before she was born.

Her stomach twisted. "Why would he have this?"

Jamie flipped the page. More notes. More scribbles. And again, like a quiet echo:

Davis.

Her hand pressed to her mouth. "He wrote my name. Before I existed."

Jamie was quiet.

She closed the journal slowly. "I don't understand."

"It doesn't mean anything bad," he said gently. "Names repeat in families. Maybe you had an ancestor named Davis. Maybe it was someone he knew."

She exhaled shakily. "Right. That makes sense."

Jamie placed a hand on top of hers.

Not grabbing.

Just touching.

"I won't let anything weird happen to you," he said softly. His thumb brushed over her skin.

She felt it everywhere.

"Jamie," she whispered.

He slowly lifted his gaze to hers.

And the air changed.

It turned electric.

Their faces were closer than they should be.

Much closer.

She didn't move.

Neither did he.

For one dangerous heartbeat, the world shrank to the distance between their mouths.

Then the chandelier flickered dramatically, because of course it did, and she jerked back like she'd been caught committing a sin.

Jamie blinked hard, jaw tightening. "Right. So. More papers."

"Yes," she squeaked. "Papers. Words. Ink. Definitely."

He scrubbed a hand over his face. "We're professionals."

"We are not," she said immediately.

"Correct," he agreed.

They sat back down, boxes between them like a barrier and a lifeline.

But nothing, not photos, not journals, not the estate, felt the same.

Things changed in a way that couldn't be denied. And he even had his shirt on.

Chapter Sixteen

JAMIE

What the hell was happening?

Jamie rubbed the back of his neck, trying to force his thoughts into something coherent, but they skittered around like a startled deer. He understood he and Davis had this odd chemistry that made no sense. The bigger problem was the *why*. And why now?

He'd found women attractive before. Plenty. But he'd never experienced this bone-deep pull, this ridiculous, persistent craving to be near someone. All. The. Time. It wasn't logical. It wasn't convenient. And it sure as hell wasn't welcome.

Davis Bernard had become an addiction.

Was it the food she made? That had to be part of it. The woman cooked like a magician, and she combined it with being a radioactive temptress. He wanted to run his fingers through her red hair and sniff. Fucking sniff for God's sake.

He'd expected to suffer through vegan meals like a monk doing penance for his sins, but instead, he was eating better than he ever had in his life. There literally was not a meal he hadn't enjoyed.

She could open a restaurant tomorrow and convert half the country to veganism. Hell, if she opened one in New York, even Wall Street carnivores would be sitting there pretending tofu was steak.

He'd hated mushrooms his whole life. They were slimy, spongy monstrosities. Yet somehow she'd tricked him into eating them disguised as "vegan chicken." And it worked. He didn't know whether to be impressed or alarmed.

And her sauces? Jesus. She could bottle those and bring nations to their knees.

Even during the sheep hunt, she'd hauled out that blasted sourdough bread and tempted him with its amazing smell. Right now, she had two loaves rising in the kitchen. The entire house smelled like yeast and heaven, and he was absolutely going to sneak a slice the moment it came out of the oven.

But food was the least of his problems.

Davis was fucking gorgeous.

Painfully, distractingly gorgeous. She caught him staring far too often, and it shocked him that she hadn't called him a creep yet. Maybe she chalked it up to hunter-brain rot. Or maybe she was being merciful.

Whatever the reason, he needed to get control of himself.

He shut his laptop harder than necessary. No point pretending he was getting any work done. He still had to finalize next month's hunt itinerary. This was a good group of familiar men. They listened, respected the wilderness, and didn't try to use their rifles like walking sticks. Easy clients.

He'd planned to leave for the trip a few days early, scout for mountain lion tracks and check water sources.

And Davis would be going with him.

Jamie ran both hands through his hair and exhaled hard.

They were alone in the house together every day. That was already too intimate for his comfort. But the wilderness? The quiet? The isolation? Sleeping in tents within arm's reach with no one around? Watching her at the campfire with her hair glowing in embers and starlight?

Nope.

No damn way he survived that intact.

The smell of fresh bread hit him before he even entered the kitchen. Warm. Tangy. Sweet. Cozy. Lethal.

His self-control didn't stand a chance.

"Stay away," Davis said immediately, pointing a spatula at him like a weapon.

"How do you expect me to stay away when it smells like that?" he countered, drifting forward on pure instinct.

She dramatically crossed the spatula-bearing hand over her chest. Her other hand pressed to her forehead. "You only love me for my bread," she moaned.

It was a joke. He knew it was a joke.

But the sound she made. That low, throaty, soft enough to be accidental sound that went straight to his groin.

Jamie's brain blanked. His breath stuttered.

Yep. He was in trouble.

"What?" she asked, blinking at him. "Do I have flour on my nose or something?"

"Or something," he managed, still staring like an idiot.

"You're making me feel self-conscious," she said with a half-grin, brushing at her cheek.

God, she had no idea. No idea what she did to him just by existing. No idea that her messy apron and wild red hair were sexier than anything in a damn Victoria's Secret catalog. No idea that her smile, unforced, warm, real, made his stomach twist in ways he didn't appreciate.

He needed distance. Space. Air. Anything, before he did something dramatically stupid.

Jamie abruptly walked to the last cupboard in the kitchen, the one where they left their car keys. He yanked his out, ignoring the way her eyes tracked him.

"I'm going for a drive," he said, trying to sound normal and failing miserably. "I'll be back in a few hours."

"Oh." She blinked, looking surprised. "Is something wrong?"

Everything, he thought.

"No," he lied. "Just need some fresh air."

He didn't look at her again. Couldn't.

If he did, he'd close the distance, grab her, and kiss her senseless. And he wasn't ready for that. She sure as hell wasn't ready for that.

So Jamie walked out the door, jaw tight, heart hammering, throat dry.

He needed a long drive and several miles between them. Okay, an entire continent would be better.

Or he was going to ruin everything.

Chapter Seventeen

DAVIS

Jamie had been acting stranger each day.

She'd started thinking he actually had a heart after the disastrous hunting trip. The way he stood between her and the brothers, the way he looked at her when he thought she wasn't paying attention. It all added up to something. But ever since they'd returned home, he'd been twitchy. Hot-and-cold like a broken faucet.

And today? Running out of the house because she moaned over bread?

That was new.

She hadn't been lying about feeling self-conscious, either. The way he looked at her sometimes, like she was something he wanted to devour but wasn't sure he was allowed to taste. It made her hot. Made a little electric sizzle spark between her thighs.

But then he'd bolt.

What was he so afraid of?

The more she thought about it, the more she realized she wanted something to happen between them. A deeper relationship? No, that wasn't the honest truth.

Sex.

Hot, mind-emptying, soul-loosening sex.

Sex to make the year go by faster. Sex that didn't have to mean anything beyond bodies and heat and relief. Her uncle hadn't said a word in his will about celibacy, so why were they acting like this?

The attraction was ridiculous. She felt it every time he walked into a room. Every time he looked at her with those intense, unguarded, dark eyes. And the look he'd given her before he fled said he felt it too.

They were adults. They could talk about this.

So why was she kneading dough like she was trying to strangle it?

Usually, the repetitive motion soothed her, but today she was wound tight and vibrating with restless energy. The bread needed another thirty minutes to rise, so she wiped her flour-covered hands and sent a text to Shady, her best friend.

Davis: hey Shady. I made it through the hunting trip and didn't kill the guide or hunters so you can spend that bail money.

Shady: I was beginning to worry. Those animal killers deserved to be boiled in oil.

Davis: They killed the most beautiful creature I've ever seen. All so they could take pictures with its dead body.

Shady: What is wrong with those sick people???

Davis: Agreed.

Shady: What about your house boy? Did his macho, I'm a great hunter schtick turn you off???

Davis: I wish. I can't do anything without picturing his abs. Each ripple is a certified weapon.

The kitchen timer beeped, cutting off her spiral. She set her phone on the dining table and returned to the kitchen to slide the risen dough into the hot oven.

Then she grabbed a towel and decided she needed a shower. Flour streaked her arms, face, and hair. She looked like she'd done battle with a bakery and lost.

Steam cleared her head a little, but not enough. Jamie shouldn't have this effect on her. He was infuriating. Arrogant. Too observant. Too attractive. Too, well, everything.

Thinking about him ruined her shower.

When she came back down, hair damp and skin still warm, she froze in the doorway.

Jamie was standing in the dining room.

Holding her phone.

She knew exactly what messages were on the screen.

"Is that my phone?" she asked.

He looked up at her, not even pretending guilt.

"You think I have sexy abs?" he asked.

Heat slammed into her cheeks so hard she nearly stumbled.

"Oh my God—" she rushed forward and snatched the phone from his hand. "You read that?!"

"I picked it up because it buzzed," he said with a shrug. "And the preview popped up."

"That does NOT give you permission—"

Stepping closer, he asked, "You wish my macho hunter schtick turned you off?"

She backed up a step, pulse skittering. "Jamie—"

He closed the distance. A predator. The mindful hunter stalking something delectable.

"And you think I have sexy abs?" he repeated, quieter now, voice dipping low.

She swallowed. "Shady's exaggerating and I don't think I said they were sexy." Had she?

"Oh, so it's an exaggeration."

"Mostly."

He arched an eyebrow. "Define mostly."

She wanted to die. Right there. Right on the antique hardwood floor.

Instead, she lifted her chin. "Why does it matter?"

He stared at her like she'd asked him the meaning of life.

Then he said hoarsely, "Because I haven't been able to stop thinking about you."

Her breath caught.

"That's why I keep running," he admitted. "I'm trying not to—" He exhaled slowly. "I'm trying not to ruin this."

"You wouldn't," she whispered.

"You don't know that."

"I do."

The air between them charged.

Jamie's eyes dropped to her mouth.

Something inside her snapped.

She stepped into him, grabbing the front of his shirt, the traitorous shirt he'd actually worn today. He inhaled sharply, the sound hungry.

"Jamie," she whispered.

That was all it took.

He kissed her.

Or she kissed him.

It happened at the same time. It was like gravity finally won the fight they'd both been resisting. His hands slid to her waist, pulling her in, anchoring her against him. His mouth captured hers with a restrained hunger that nearly buckled her knees.

Her fingers fisted in his shirt, pulling him closer, needing more. Needing all of him.

He kissed like he'd wanted this for days.

Weeks.

Like he was starved.

He angled her head, deepening the kiss, tasting her with a slow, deliberate intensity that sent heat spiraling through her in dizzying waves. She gasped softly against his mouth, and he groaned, an unguarded sound that made her entire body shiver.

When they finally broke apart, foreheads touching, both of them breathless and stunned, Jamie whispered: "This is why I ran."

She brushed her lips over his again. "This is why you shouldn't."

His laugh was soft and pained. "Davis," he groaned.

She smiled, eyes half-lidded. "Stop thinking."

He kissed her again. Longer. Deeper. With less restraint and more certainty.

And for the first time since arriving at her uncle's estate, Davis stopped wondering if they could survive a year together.

His hand slid to her breast.

"Yes," she whispered.

"Yes," he whispered back.

And the bread timer went off.

"Leave it," he said.

"The bread will burn and be worthless."

"In that case, rescue it immediately."

She saw the smile in his eyes. "I told you. You only love me for my bread."

"I didn't deny it."

Chapter Eighteen

JAMIE

They didn't kiss again for five days.

Five days of pretending it hadn't happened. Five days of him remembering every second of it. Five days of trying and failing to act like a functional human being instead of a man who'd tasted something he wanted more than oxygen.

He didn't understand why they hadn't fallen into bed immediately. They should've been tangled in sheets by now, breathing hard, laughing, unable to keep their hands off each other.

Instead, she avoided him in the subtlest ways; turning her face when he walked into the room, keeping conversations light and quick, ducking around corners like he was dangerous.

Maybe he was.

Maybe he'd scared her.

His preparations for the next hunt were finished. Maps finalized, coordinates logged, gear packed. They'd leave next week. Normally, he liked the anticipation of a trip. He liked knowing the wilderness was waiting for him.

But this time, the only thing he could think about was her.

And then the storm hit.

It came in fast. Thick clouds rolling in from the mountains, the sky bruising purple, wind slicing through the trees. Jamie was in the mudroom checking gear when the first crack of thunder shook the house.

He heard Davis's footsteps upstairs.

And then a deafening boom.

A tree crashed somewhere on the property. The whole house shuddered like it took a punch to the ribs.

"Davis!" he called, already moving.

No answer.

He sprinted up the stairs, taking them two at a time as another roll of thunder cracked the sky open. Wind howled against the house. Something thumped. Maybe it was a branch hitting the roof.

He found her standing at the window of the landing, her palms pressed to the glass.

A massive pine had fallen near the house. It didn't hit directly, but it was too close for comfort.

"Hey," he said, coming up beside her. "You okay?"

She startled, then nodded too quickly. "I'm fine. I just. It was loud."

"Yeah," he said softly. "Come away from the window."

She let him guide her back, but her arms shook. And he knew. She was as worried about him as she was the storm. There had been too much quiet between them. Too much unsaid. Five full days of suspended breath.

A particularly violent crack of thunder made her flinch hard, and the sound ripped through him. He reached out instinctively, hands settling on her upper arms.

"Davis," he murmured, "look at me."

She did.

God, her eyes.

She looked scared and frustrated and like she was trying so hard not to unravel. The storm outside rattled the old house again, and windows trembled in their frames.

He brushed his thumb along her arm. "You're safe."

She swallowed. "I know."

"Then what is it?"

Her breath hitched.

"Jamie," she whispered, "I'm tired of pretending that kiss didn't happen."

His pulse slammed into overdrive. "Me too."

"I don't want to ignore it," she said, voice trembling with something far bigger than fear. "I don't want to pretend I don't think about it every night."

He stepped closer. Barely an inch. Enough to feel the heat of her skin.

"And what do you think about?" he asked quietly.

Her breath shivered out. "You."

His self-control snapped like the tree outside.

He took her face in both hands. "Davis, tell me to stop."

"I won't."

Lightning flashed, lighting the hallway in stark white.

He kissed her.

This time it wasn't tentative or careful. This was weeks of tension breaking open, all heat and desperation and want. Her fingers curled around his shoulders, pulling him closer, and he backed her gently against the wall as thunder shook the house again.

She tasted like sugar and spice and something he hadn't let himself hope for.

Her soft lips parted under his, and he deepened the kiss, feeling her melt into him. Her hands slid up the back of his neck, grip tightening as another thunderclap cracked the air.

He pressed his forehead to hers. Both of them breathing hard. The storm roared outside. But inside, everything narrowed to just them.

Her voice was a whisper, shaking with want. "Jamie, don't run from me again."

"Not a chance," he rasped.

The lights flickered.

She pulled him toward her bedroom.

He followed.

Their mouths found each other again, more urgent this time. His hands slid to her hips, her fingers threaded into his hair, and they stumbled together through the doorway as a new storm raged inside.

He kicked the door shut behind them.

The world fell away.

What happened next was heat, need, and the kind of intimacy that had been building from the first moment she walked into that house and saw him naked.

They didn't come together in a frenzy.

They came together like gravity. Inevitable, consuming, and unstoppable.

As the storm pounded the estate, they finally stopped pretending.

Thunder cracked. The noise jolted through the floorboards, through the walls, through her, but Jamie's hands at her waist held her safe.

He kissed her again, slower this time, deeper. A claiming, a question, and an answer all at once.

His voice was low and rough against her mouth. "You sure about this?"

She nodded, brushing her lips over his in a trembling whisper. "I've been sure for days."

The admission hit him like a blow. Something strained and hungry flickered across his face before he cupped her cheek with a tenderness that made her knees weaken.

Lightning flashed again, illuminating him in sharp lines; broad shoulders, storm-shadowed bushy jaw, soft eyes that contradicted everything he pretended to be.

"Then come here," he murmured.

He kissed her again. Slow at first, then with a growing urgency as she fisted her hands in his shirt, pulling him closer until there was no space left at all. He tasted like heat with restraint fraying at the edges.

When he slid his hands up her spine, every nerve ending woke up at once.

She broke the kiss long enough to whisper, breathless, "Jamie."

He froze, not pulling away, but pausing, searching her face like she held the only answer he cared about.

"I don't want to rush you," he said, his thumb brushing her jaw. "Tell me what you want."

A shiver ran through her. Not from the storm, not from fear, but from the sheer care in his voice. She hadn't expected that. Not from him. Not from a man made of wilderness, iron, and stubbornness.

"I want you," she breathed. "I've wanted you since the moment you ran from me like a coward."

He huffed out a strained laugh. "Only ran because I wanted this too much."

"Then stop running."

He kissed her again. It was the kind of kiss that wiped every coherent thought from her mind. His hands slid down her sides almost worshipful, before settling on her hips like he was memorizing the feel of her.

She tugged at his shirt, and he lifted his arms to let her pull it off. The lightning outside lit his skin in flashes. He was warm and solid and entirely too beautiful.

Davis's breath caught.

Jamie watched her watching him, chest rising and falling quickly. "You look at me like that," he warned softly, "and I'm not going to make it to the bed."

Her pulse skipped. "Then don't."

He kissed her again, deeper this time, guiding her backward until her legs brushed the mattress. His mouth trailed along her jaw and she tilted her head instinctively, breath catching at the warmth of him against her neck.

"Davis," he murmured against her skin, saying her name like it meant something.

She slid her hands over his shoulders, feeling muscles shift under her palms, and he drew in a sharp breath like her touch did something to him he wasn't prepared for.

His forehead pressed to hers. "Tell me if it's too much. At any point."

"It won't be."

"I mean it."

She lifted his chin so he had to look her in the eyes. "Jamie, I want this. I want you."

The air between them tightened further, pulled taut by something deeper than lust, heavier than want.

He kissed her again, and this time it was undeniable. This was happening because neither of them could stop it anymore, because it had been building from the moment she barged into his bedroom and found him naked.

He lowered her gently onto the bed, following her down, his body braced so his weight didn't crush her. Another thunderclap boomed, and she flinched, just barely, but he caught her gaze and kissed her again.

"You're safe," he whispered.

"I know."

"You're with me."

"I know."

She curled her fingers into his hair. "Jamie, stop talking."

He laughed quietly and kissed her again, and the storm outside raged on as they sank into the heat and the softness and the inevitability of each other.

He touched her like she was something precious. Not fragile, not breakable, but wanted. And she pulled him closer because she'd been waiting for this exact moment to finally happen.

The world narrowed to warmth and breath and whispered names.

Then the storm swallowed the rest.

His hands slid up her sides, hesitant at first, then surer when she arched into his touch. When he finally cupped her breasts through the thin fabric of her shirt, she let out a sound that made them both freeze. It was a cross between shock, hunger, and realization.

Too many clothes.

Far too many.

They moved at the same moment, hands tugging, pulling, fumbling in their urgency. Her shirt lifted, tangled, dropped to the floor. Her fingers brushed his skin, and he inhaled sharply. Pants were shoved down; underthings followed. A tangle of limbs, soft laughs, soft curses, heat rising between them like the storm outside had moved into the room.

When he settled over her again, his hands were everywhere. Her waist, her hips, the curve of her stomach, the delicate line of her neck. Every touch was searching and hungry all at once.

She arched to meet him, needing him closer, needing everything he was giving and everything he was holding back.

Then her need shifted. "Please," she whispered into his mouth, the word shaking between them.

Jamie went still, bracing above her, his forehead pressed to hers. His eyes burned dark, tender in a way that made her chest tighten.

"I've waited so long for this," he murmured.

She nodded, opening herself to him, trusting him in a way that felt terrifying and right.

He kissed her once before his body lowered toward hers, pressing into her warmth, her readiness. She gasped at the newness of him, the weight, the closeness, the overwhelming sense of finality.

Her hands roamed over him hungrily now. His back and his shoulders as the lines of muscle shifted beneath her fingertips. She wanted to memorize all of him. Wanted him pressed against her, around her, inside her, until the storm had nothing on them.

He moved with a careful patience at first, checking her breath, her reactions, the way her fingers tightened against his skin. When she lifted her hips to meet him, any restraint he had left slipped.

Their rhythm grew more intimate, the kind of closeness that made her feel like she was unraveling and finding herself at the same time. His breath mingled with hers. Sweat slicked their skin, sliding between them as they moved together in a way that felt instinctive and inevitable.

The need inside her tightened, coiled, burned hotter with each slow press of his body to hers. She clung to him, wanting more, wanting him everywhere, wanting this moment to stretch and stretch until time forgot itself.

He whispered her name again.

She answered with a soft cry, her body rising to meet his, matching him, urging him on.

They chased the moment together, both breathless, shaking, not wanting to reach the end but helpless against how quickly it was building, how right it felt.

And when it finally broke over them, it wasn't just release.

It was surrender.

It was everything they hadn't said. Everything they'd tried to avoid. Everything they couldn't run from anymore.

Chapter Nineteen

DAVIS

Davis woke before Jamie.

That was new.

Sunlight filtered weakly through the curtains, the storm finally exhausted after tearing half the property to shreds. Her body felt warm and pleasantly heavy in ways she hadn't experienced in a long time. The sheets smelled like him. Pine and something quietly masculine that made her want to bury her face in the pillow he was using.

He had one arm draped across her waist, as he breathed lightly against her shoulder.

Last night rushed back in waves. The lightning, the crash of the tree, his hands on her, his voice saying, *tell me to stop*, her saying *I won't*, and everything that followed.

Heat flooded her cheeks.

Holy.

Actual.

Hell.

She had sex with him. Three times throughout the night. And he had stayed. Held her. Like she mattered.

The realization was so startling her breath caught in her throat.

Her last romantic fling had lasted four months. The one before that, six. Neither man cared enough to stick around when she started feeling suffocated. She'd never felt as connected to them as she did to Jamie. They had nothing in common. They were literally from two different solar systems. And she didn't care. They had the rest of their year together. They would likely fight during most of it. She looked at him. She could handle the disagreements, especially if they ended in one bed. No emotional entanglement, just burning-hot sex to relieve their tension. That's what she needed.

He shifted then, tightening his arm around her. His face nuzzled the back of her shoulder. Intimate.

Too intimate.

"Oh no," she whispered.

This was dangerous. Sex she could compartmentalize. Attraction she could handle. But waking up tangled together, wrapped in silence and sunlight and sex smells?

That was how people fell.

She carefully slid out from under his arm, trying not to wake him. Jamie made a quiet, half-asleep sound of protest, but didn't open his eyes. She slipped on leggings and a sweatshirt and escaped the room before she did something ridiculous like crawl back into bed with him.

Downstairs, the scent of the storm still lingered as she stepped outside.

A huge pine lay across the edge of the lawn, fractured into ugly angles. Roof shingles littered the ground. A decorative shutter dangled crookedly on its mount.

She sighed. "Oh great. The apocalypse came early."

The door creaked behind her.

Jamie's voice, still gravelly with sleep: "You should still be in bed."

She turned.

He stood barefoot on the porch, hair tousled, shirtless, because of course he was, and looking entirely too good for someone who had ruined her ability to form coherent thought.

"You scared me," she said.

"You ran off," he countered gently. "I woke up cold."

Her face heated. "You were practically glued to me."

He smirked. "Good, hot glue."

She rolled her eyes because the alternative was melting into a puddle.

He stepped beside her, squinting at the fallen tree. "Minimal damage. Could've been worse."

"Could've smashed the house."

"Could've smashed you," he murmured, eyes drifting to her face with a softness she wasn't ready for.

She swallowed. "Well, it didn't."

"We should clean up the yard before the next storm rolls in."

"Another storm?"

"Clouds say yes."

She stared at him. "You can read clouds?"

"I can read you better."

Her pulse tripped over itself. "That's not hard. I'm in a state of shock."

Jamie didn't smile. Instead, he tenderly brushed a fallen leaf from her hair.

"About last night—" he began.

"Nope," she blurted. "No talking until we clean up. Manual labor first. Emotional crisis second."

His lips curved. "You're cute when you panic."

"I'm not panicking."

"You're very panicking."

She pointed at the debris. "Pick up branches or I'm going back to bed."

"Your bed or mine?" he said far too casually.

She nearly threw a branch at him.

But then he bent down beside her to gather fallen limbs, and something shifted again. Domestic bliss? Familiar. A quiet kind of intimacy wrapped in mundane tasks. She almost pulled a "Jamie" and bolted.

They worked side by side, moving branches into piles, inspecting the house, climbing onto the porch railing so Jamie could reattach the shutter while she steadied him by the waistband of his jeans.

"Careful," she said.

"I've got balance."

"Humor me."

He glanced down and didn't say the smart remark on his lips. Instead, he said softly, "I like this."

"Fixing storm damage?"

"No." He hopped down beside her, closer than before. "Doing something normal with you."

It shouldn't have made her chest feel warm. It shouldn't have made her breath catch. But it did. Sex, she reminded herself. Just sex.

They gathered debris in silence for a while until Jamie brushed his fingers against hers. "Davis," he said quietly.

"Mm?"

"About last night..." He hesitated. "I don't regret it."

She swallowed hard. "Me neither."

Relief washed over his face.

"But," she added quickly, "I don't want to rush into anything complicated."

He nodded. "Then we won't."

"But we're not ignoring it either."

"No," he said. "Definitely not ignoring it."

A soft wind rustled the broken branches around them.

Then, unexpectedly, Jamie reached out and threaded his fingers through hers.

Not possessive. Not claiming. Just holding.

Davis froze. "Jamie."

"You can pull away," he said, thumb brushing her knuckles. "If it's too much."

She didn't pull away.

She squeezed back.

Just once. Just enough.

And his exhale sounded like something unwound inside him.

They stood like that for a long moment, hands clasped, storm debris around them, the whole world hushed by the aftermath.

She finally whispered, "We should finish cleaning."

He didn't let go. "Yeah," he said softly. "We should."

But he didn't move. Not yet.

Neither did she.

Chapter Twenty

DAVIS

Davis had never feared death until the moment she saw the aircraft.

Calling it a plane was generous. It was more like an aluminum soda can with wings. The propeller looked older than her kindergarten certificate. The pilot wore an expression that said he'd seen things humans weren't meant to witness and survived only out of spite. He also looked a few days past ninety.

"You're kidding," Davis whispered as she approached.

Jamie slung his pack over his shoulder, completely unbothered. "It's safe."

"This thing?" She pointed at the plane and didn't mention the age of the pilot because he was standing too close.

"This thing is one bird sneeze away from spontaneous disassembly."

"It's flown for decades."

"That is not a reassuring sentence."

The pilot spat a sunflower seed onto the ground. Licked his finger and checked the wind direction. "She'll fly fine," he said in a gravelly voice that suggested he'd smoked since the womb. "Unless the wind picks up. Or the left engine stalls. But even then—"

Davis slapped her palms over her ears. "Nope. No thank you. I don't need details."

Jamie smirked. "It'll be a quick flight."

"Define quick," she said skeptically.

"Two hours."

"Two hours? In that?"

"Do you want to fly for ninety minutes, then hike twenty-six miles to the drop-off instead?"

She glared. He had a point. A horrible one.

"Fine." She exhaled deeply. "But if I die, please tell Shady I hold her morally responsible for encouraging my acceptance of the will."

"I can't believe you have a best friend named Shady. Do you call her Slim when she's being ornery?"

"Haha," Davis said. "Too bad it didn't work to distract me."

Jamie opened the plane door for her in a mock gentlemanly gesture. "After you."

"I hate you," she muttered, climbing in.

"I know," he said, climbing in after her. "You've said it at least a thousand times."

When the plane took off, Davis grabbed the sides of her seat so hard she nearly tore the fabric. The turbulence was immediate. The aircraft rattled like someone had put it together using dental floss and bubblegum.

Jamie reached over and took her hand.

She didn't pull away.

"You're okay," he murmured.

"No, I'm not," she whispered through clenched teeth. "This plane is held together with duct tape." She said it to be generous.

He squeezed her fingers gently. "Then I'll hold you together."

Okay. That helped a little.

Jamie swore it was two hours, but the trip seemed like twenty. Jamie had to remind her to breathe constantly. She didn't think it would ever end.

The "landing runway" was a strip of dirt in the middle of nowhere, surrounded by thick forest and mountains that looked like they'd eaten something wild for breakfast.

The pilot waved casually as they unloaded their gear. "I'll be back in five days to pick you up."

"What?" Davis shouted.

But he'd already closed the cockpit. She watched as he took off in a gust of dust and noise. The moment the plane disappeared into the sky, the world turned too quiet.

Jamie inhaled deeply, hands on his hips. "Perfect weather for scouting."

"Perfect weather for a breakdown," she muttered.

The air was crisp, the forest dense, the mountains rising high against the afternoon sun. It was breathtaking. Like a postcard that wanted to kill you.

They hiked for an hour before stopping near a creek.

"The hunters will meet us here in three days."

That gave Davis time to plan her sabotage.

Jamie crouched near the bank, pointing at a set of fresh tracks. "See this? Mountain lion. Big one."

She crouched beside him, studying the impression more closely. Her stomach twisted, not out of fear, but out of guilt.

A beautiful animal lived near here. She wasn't about to aid trophy hunters in killing it, even if the lion scared the snot out of her.

Jamie looked up, brow furrowing. "You okay?"

"I'm great," she lied. "Totally calm. Definitely not thinking murderous thoughts about the hunters who are meeting you."

"That tracks." He stood and continued along the creek bed, scanning for signs of activity. Davis followed.

And every time she spotted something that could be a track, she smudged it with the toe of her boot.

Casual.

Innocent.

Erased.

Jamie pointed at another spot. "Look there. The ridge is perfect for scouting. The hunters will—"

Smudge.

He frowned. "Did you just—?"

"Nope. That wasn't me. Must've been wind. Or erosion. Or tiny erosion elves."

"Erosion elves?"

"They're rare. Look it up."

He stared at her suspiciously, but kept moving. She stayed behind him.

The next set of would be tracks she wiped with a stick while pretending to admire moss.

The next she covered with loose leaves.

The next she subtly pushed water over with her boot.

After the fourth one, Jamie stopped walking entirely.

He crossed his arms.

"Davis."

She froze mid-sabotage, boot still hovering over a very clear paw print.

"I can explain," she said.

"Can you?"

"Yes."

"I'd love to hear it."

"Um, I was stretching?"

He gave her the slowest, longest, most unimpressed blink in human history.

"You're sabotaging the hunt."

"What? No. Sabotage is intentional. This is an accident. A series of accidents. Unrelated accidents."

"Accidents that only affect animal tracks?"

"Yes," she said, nodding convincingly. "Very track-specific accidents."

He sighed, pinching the bridge of his nose. "Davis."

"No, listen," she said, stepping closer. "I know this is your job. I know you love the outdoors. But I can't just stand here while people come out to shoot something simply because they want it stuffed on their wall."

"I get that."

Her mouth fell open. "You do?"

"I don't like trophy hunting either," he admitted quietly. "I guide the hunts because it's work, not because they all make me happy."

That stopped her cold.

He continued, "These animals. I respect them. More than the men who shoot them half the time."

"Then why do you—"

"Because guide work doesn't pay much unless you take everything that comes your way. Even the stuff you don't like."

She stared at him.

He wasn't lying. She could hear it in his voice.

"Jamie," she whispered.

He took her hand, surprising her. "I'm not going to be mad at you for caring."

"I'm not trying to ruin your job."

He gave a half-smile. "You already did."

"Oh God. I'm sorry."

"Davis." He tugged her closer. "I'm kidding."

Her breath caught.

His thumb brushed her knuckles. "But please don't destroy the tracks," he added gently. "We still need to lead them somewhere safe."

"Safe for the hunters?"

"Safe for the cats."

Emotion pricked behind her ribs.

She nodded. "Okay. Deal."

They walked on for several steps before she realized their hands were still joined.

Chapter Twenty-One

JAMIE

Jamie had slept in tents hundreds of times.

Alone.

With clients.

With loud snorers.

With panicked rookies.

With men he barely tolerated.

But he had never shared a tent with someone who made his pulse skip like Davis did.

And now she was sitting cross-legged on his sleeping mat, hair loose after the long hike, cheeks flushed with cold and a little exertion, the lantern light turning her skin golden.

His heartbeat was somewhere in the vicinity of too damn loud.

Davis looked around the cramped space and raised one eyebrow. "This tent is tiny."

"It's ultralight," he said. "Hikers love them." He'd only packed the one tent but he wouldn't tell her that unless she asked.

"Hikers who travel alone." She gestured at the narrow space. "This is a single person sleeping pad."

He cleared his throat. "Yeah."

Her eyes flicked up to his. "Are we sleeping like sardines? Or is someone sleeping outside with the wolves?"

"You're not sleeping outside."

"I wasn't offering me," she said dryly.

"I'm not sleeping outside either," he said. "Wolves like me too much."

She scoffed. "That's not reassuring."

He was suddenly hyper-aware of the fact that in another thirty seconds they would officially be lying down together. In a tent. In the dark. With no space to pretend he wasn't dying to touch her again.

She noticed the tension. Of course she did.

"Jamie," she said softly, studying him, "you okay?"

No. Absolutely not.

But he nodded anyway. "Just tired."

She slowly crawled closer until her knee touched his. "You get quiet," she said, tilting her head, "when you're worried."

"What makes you think I'm worried?"

"You didn't make one sarcastic comment about me nearly tripping over that log."

"I was busy making sure you didn't actually fall."

She smiled. "You take care of me."

He swallowed hard. "Someone has to."

Her eyes softened further. "You want me close?" she asked quietly.

He didn't answer with words.

He leaned in and kissed her.

This one was slow. Not like the storm kiss, which had been wild and fierce. And not like the first kiss, which had been filled with shock and hunger. This was a quiet pull between them, like something inevitable drawing them together in the dim lantern glow.

Her fingers slid up his jaw. His hands found her hips. She climbed into his lap without him asking, knees bracketing his waist, and he exhaled against her mouth like she'd knocked the air straight from him.

The kiss deepened. It was soft, then warmer, then heated in the way two people starved for each other slipped back into easily. But they didn't rush. They didn't tear at clothing. They moved together in slow, savoring touches, foreheads pressed together between kisses.

Her lips brushed his ear. "Jamie," she whispered.

He shivered.

They lay down together, tangled but gentle, her head on his shoulder, her leg hooked over his, her fingers drawing soft circles on his chest. The closeness felt intimate in a different way. It had less fire with more certainty. More, *them*.

A few more kisses followed as they explored the familiar heat. It never crossed into urgency. Just enough to leave them breathless and wanting without losing themselves completely until they did.

Clothing came off, heat increased, moans and sighs filled the tent. It was perfect. He loved the sounds she made when she came.

She finally settled against him murmuring, "I like this."

His chest tightened. "Me too."

Silence stretched between them.

Until Davis whispered, "Jamie, can I ask you something?"

"Anything."

"Why did my uncle write the will the way he did?"

He hesitated, not because he didn't want to answer, but because the question hit deeper than he expected.

"I've been thinking about that too," he admitted.

"You have?"

"Yeah," he said softly. "A lot."

She shifted so she could see him better in the dim light. "Tell me."

He brushed a strand of hair behind her ear. "Your uncle wasn't stupid. Reclusive, yes. Odd, definitely. But not stupid."

"That's not exactly comforting," she muttered.

He smiled faintly. "I mean he didn't choose us randomly. He didn't create those rules because he was bored. I think he wanted something."

"Like what?"

"Balance, maybe," Jamie said. "You and me? We're opposites. Total opposites. But somehow," he exhaled, "we make each other better."

She blinked, surprised. "You think I make you better?"

"Davis," he said gently, "you've changed the way I see everything. Food. Hunting. People. Myself."

Her breath caught.

"And I'm trying, God knows I'm trying, because I want to keep up with you."

She stared at him like he'd spoken a language she didn't know she understood.

"Your turn," he said quietly. "How have I made you better?"

Her throat tightened. "You protect me. Even when you think I don't notice."

He didn't speak, waiting.

"And you make me brave," she whispered. "Even when I'm terrified. You make me feel like I can do things I'd never try alone."

Jamie swallowed hard, his heart pounding in his chest. "I think that's why your uncle chose this. He wanted us to pull each other out of the corners we hide in."

"That's a lot of faith in someone who didn't even know us," she murmured.

"He had to have believed something good would come of it."

"Do you?" she asked.

He brushed his thumb across her cheek. "Yeah. I do."

She lowered her head and kissed him again. This time it was slow, grateful, and tender.

He pulled her closer, arms wrapping around her.

The lantern flickered, casting light across the tent's fabric.

Outside, the wilderness was silent.

Inside, wrapped in each other, they were anything but.

Chapter Twenty-Two

JAMIE

He heard them before he saw them.

Three booming voices arguing with the enthusiasm of men who had absolutely no idea how loud they were in the wilderness. Branches snapped. Rocks tumbled. Someone swore about "that damn pack mule of a backpack."

Jamie sighed. *Here we go.*

Davis looked at him from the tent entrance, eyebrows raised. "Are those the hunters or drunk bears?"

"Hunters," he confirmed. "Very loud hunters."

"Oh good," she deadpanned. "I was worried the wildlife wouldn't hear them coming."

The bushes shook violently, and the first man stumbled through: Bo Hardy, tall, good-natured, built like a linebacker with a permanent sunburn. Behind him came Clayton "Clay" Stonely, who looked like he'd stepped out of an L.L. Bean catalog but smelled like yesterday's chili. Lastly was Nate Puckett, the youngest, wiry, excitable, and constantly narrating his own survival show despite not being filmed.

"CALL-O-WAY!" Bo bellowed. "You beautiful bastard!"

Jamie braced himself. Bo scooped him into a back-crushing hug.

Davis mouthed, *Oh my God.*

Clay slapped Jamie on the shoulder. "Good to see you, man. You ready for round four?"

"Always am," Jamie said diplomatically. "How was the flight?"

Nate dropped his pack dramatically. "I thought we were gonna die. The pilot sneezed and the whole plane swerved."

Bo waved him off. "He's exaggerating. It was only mild turbulence. Don't make us sound wimpy in front of—"

Bo stopped. Squinted.

His eyebrows slowly rose as he regarded Davis.

"Uh, Jamie?" Bo glanced between them. "You brought a girl?"

Here we go.

Clay stepped forward, blinking in confusion. "Is she, uh, like someone's girlfriend? Or is she lost?"

Nate whispered loudly, "Do we rescue her or is she part of the adventure package?"

Davis crossed her arms. "I'm not lost. And I don't need rescue. You might though if one of you tries to mansplain tying shoelaces."

Nate straightened. "I feel threatened."

Jamie stepped between them before someone got eaten alive, probably Nate. "Guys, this is Davis. She's shadowing me for the year."

Clay coughed. "Shadowing."

Bo lowered his voice. "On a man trip?"

"It's a hunting trip," Jamie corrected.

"Exactly," Bo said. "A man trip."

Davis arched an eyebrow. "Fascinating. Do testicles improve your hunting ability?"

Nate choked. Clay snorted. Bo turned purple trying not to laugh.

Jamie hid his smile behind his hand.

He should not find her this attractive while she verbally dismantled three grown men. But here they were.

Bo cleared his throat. "Uh, well. Welcome then. Didn't know we'd have company. Especially not female company," he said under his breath.

Nate stepped forward suddenly, offering his hand. "I'm Nate. I don't usually sweat this much, it's the altitude."

"It's the chili," Clay muttered.

Davis shook his hand politely. "Nice to meet you. Is this your first hunt?"

Nate puffed up. "Fourth. Last year I got a sixteen-pointer."

Davis smiled sweetly. "I'm sure it was thrilled to die for you."

Nate deflated. "Oh. Uh."

Bo dragged him away before he said anything else. "Ignore him. His language skills need help."

Clay raised a brow at Jamie. "You sure she can handle the hike?"

Jamie didn't even glance back. "She handled yesterday's better than any of you three ever have."

Clay grinned. "Oh, she's one of those."

"One of what?" Davis asked, narrowing her eyes.

"Nuclear fit," Clay said. "The worst kind. Makes the rest of us look bad."

Davis smirked. "Then yes, I'm absolutely one of those."

Jamie ran a hand through his hair. "All right, listen. We'll set up camp, go over the plan for tomorrow, and get an early night. Big day ahead."

Bo nodded, then cupped his hands around his mouth. "Hey Jamie, does she know we're hunting mountain lions?"

Davis stopped dead.

Jamie shot Bo a look that could melt steel. "No. And we're not."

"Thought the permit—"

Jamie cut him off sharply. "We're not hunting cats."

Bo blinked. "We're not?"

"No. Elk. They sent the wrong permits."

Clay shrugged. "Fine by me. Cats creep me out. All spines and eyes."

Nate shivered. "They look into your soul."

"They judge your soul," Davis said. "I've seen it."

All three hunters stared at her for a collective moment.

Jamie seized the opportunity. "So nobody takes a shot tomorrow without my say-so."

They nodded fervently.

Davis walked past them toward the creek, whispering just loud enough for Jamie to hear, "If any of them even think about shooting a mountain lion, I'm smudging everything except their own footprints. I'm not happy at all about the elk either."

"I'm a hunting guide," he said in exasperation.

She flicked a glance at him over her shoulder.

The guys kept unpacking, muttering among themselves:

Bo: "She's scary."

Clay: "She's funny."

Nate: "She glared at me. I think she cursed me."

Bo: "You'll be fine. Maybe."

And Jamie. He realized something unsettling.

He liked having her here.

He liked her shaking the guys up.

He liked her fire and her conviction and the way she made even seasoned hunters step carefully.

He liked her more than he should.

"Dude," Clay said suddenly, elbowing him, "you're staring."

Jamie jerked. "Shut up."

Clay grinned. "Oh man. You're in trouble."

Yeah.

He was.

Chapter Twenty-Three

DAVIS

She was no crazier about killing an elk than killing a mountain lion.

In her mind, one had antlers, the other had claws, and both had done absolutely nothing to deserve being hunted by three grown men who couldn't find a track if it came with neon arrows and a map labeled, *You Are Here, Genius.*

But she also wasn't stupid.

Elk were quieter, faster, harder to accidentally run into. Mountain lions, well, those had opinions about being disturbed.

Elk it was.

Still didn't mean she wanted one dead. Just the thought made her stomach turn.

The next morning, Jamie led the group along a ridge overlooking a valley that looked like a painting with golden grass, patches of evergreens, and sunlight bouncing off the river like someone had spilled diamonds downstream. It was gorgeous.

And she was absolutely going to ruin everything.

She walked behind the men, hands casually tucked into her pink pack straps, doing her best innocent face. Jamie had given her the look earlier. It was the one that said, *Don't get me fired, don't get me arrested, and don't antagonize the guys carrying rifles.*

She nodded sweetly.

And then immediately resumed her sabotage scheming.

Bo stopped to point at what he thought were elk tracks. "Boys, look at this. Big ones."

Davis discreetly stepped forward and scuffed the dirt with her boot.

Nate leaned over. "Wait Bo, these look mushy?"

"They're not mushy," Bo insisted. "They're fresh."

Jamie approached, kneeling beside them. He pressed a thumb along the edge of one track.

Then he looked up at her.

Very slowly.

She smiled brightly. "Nature is so magical."

Jamie inhaled. He stood, dusting his hands off. "They're partially degraded. Could be wind, rain, or careless foot traffic."

This was said with the calm disappointment of a man who knew exactly who the careless foot traffic was.

Clay frowned. "So no elk?"

"Not those ones," Jamie said, giving her a *Behave* look.

Davis gave him a *Make me* look.

The hunt moved on.

A few minutes later, they entered a narrow clearing where elk often passed through. Jamie crouched again, scanning the ground.

"You hear that?" Nate asked suddenly.

They all paused.

The forest was silent.

Too silent.

Good.

Perfect for interference.

"Dude," Bo whispered. "I think I heard something big."

"You did," Davis said, clearing her throat.

Then she shouldered off her pack, reached inside, and extricated two pans, which she slammed together like a deranged cymbalist.

"RAAAAAANG!"

Every creature within three square miles fled the planet.

Nate nearly fell over. "What the fuck?"

"Sorry!" Davis said. "Dropped them!"

Jamie stared at her like she had just personally offended his ancestors.

"Dropped them?" he echoed.

"Yes," she said innocently. "Accidentally. Twice."

More *clang clang* noises happened as she attempted to shove the pots back in her pack. The noise was definitely intentional.

Jamie pinched the bridge of his nose so hard she thought he'd leave a thumbprint.

Clay sighed. "Well, the elk are definitely gone now."

Bo nodded sagely. "Probably ran to Utah."

"Or Canada," Nate added.

"Or Mars," Davis suggested helpfully.

Jamie muttered something under his breath that sounded like, "You're going to kill me before the hunters even try to."

An hour later, Jamie found more elk sign.

Fresh.

Not yet trampled by Davis.

He looked at her slowly. "Davis. Don't."

She jutted her chin out. "I'm not doing anything."

"You're thinking about doing something."

"No, I'm thinking biblical thoughts."

"We're in a national forest, not a church."

She stuck her tongue out at him when the guys weren't looking.

Jamie's lips twitched.

The men crouched to examine the prints more closely. Davis wandered toward a nearby tree.

She waited until they all gathered, whispering about wind direction and shot angles.

Then she took a deep breath and blew the world's loudest, shrillest, most horrifying note through the emergency whistle Jamie had given her on their first hunt.

FWEEEEEEEEEEEEEET!

Birds exploded out of trees.

Squirrels fled.

The men dove for cover.

"What the hell was that?!" Bo shouted.

"My safety whistle," Davis said cheerfully. "Jamie said I should test my equipment."

Jamie stood there, staring at her in exhausted disbelief.

"I didn't say to test it during a stalk."

"Oh," she said. "Should I wait until we're closer next time?"

Clay groaned. "We're never getting an elk."

Nate collapsed dramatically. "We're doomed."

Bo wiped his face. "Calloway, can we fire her?"

Davis gasped loudly. "Jamie! Did you hear that? They're union busting!"

"We're not unionizing," Jamie muttered.

"We should!" she said, placing her hands on her hips. "Solidarity now. Equal rights for all animals. No hunting."

Bo stared at her. "Lady, you're terrifying."

She beamed.

The group finally moved on, the hunters frustrated, the forest empty of anything with legs except them.

Davis walked beside Jamie now, a little sheepish.

"You mad?" she asked.

He shook his head. "No."

"You sure?"

He stopped walking.

Turned toward her.

And leaned down until his mouth was beside her ear.

His voice was a little rougher than usual.

"I'm not mad," he murmured. "I'm completely, utterly, painfully in love with your chaos."

Her breath hitched.

"And I really need you to stop using your whistle unless you're in danger," he added, slightly louder.

"Okay," she whispered.

"Also," he said, "stop kicking elk tracks."

"No promises."

He smiled.

She smiled back.

Behind them, Nate complained loudly, "Why does the forest hate us?"

Davis whispered, "Because it has taste."

Jamie laughed under his breath.

She reached for his hand.

He let her take it.

Chapter Twenty-Four

DAVIS

By the time the sun started dipping behind the tree line, even Davis had to admit the hunters looked defeated.

And tired.

And mildly traumatized by her sabotage.

Clay dragged himself into camp like a wounded dog. Nate collapsed on a log, dramatically clutching his chest. Bo sighed as he dropped his pack with a heavy thud.

Jamie, to his credit, did not scold her.

Yet.

The fire crackled while darkness slowly pulled itself across the valley. Somewhere in the distance, an owl called.

Davis sat on a log next to Jamie, stirring her pot of lentil stew, the least offensive vegan meal she could produce without revealing her ongoing "anti-hunt rebellion."

Bo sniffed. "Smells good."

Clay sniffed harder. "Yeah, it actually does."

Nate leaned over her shoulder. "Is that food food?"

She arched a brow. "Do you want some or not?"

Nate put both hands up. "Oh, absolutely. I'm accustomed to canned food on a hunt, not real food."

Davis smirked. "Try to contain your shock."

Jamie nudged her gently. "Be nice."

"I am being nice. I'm sharing food. That's the nicest thing a human can do in the woods."

Nate took a tentative bite and blinked rapidly. "Holy cow, this is delicious." Then he tasted the wedge of bread she'd included. "Oh my God. I'm in heaven."

Bo ladled himself a bowl. "Calloway, you're in trouble."

Jamie looked up. "Huh?"

Bo pointed his spoon at Davis. "This one? She's marriage material and I just might."

Davis choked on her own laughter. "Please don't propose. I'm taken."

Jamie's spoon froze midair.

Clay looked between them. "Wait, taken by who?"

She gestured vaguely toward Jamie. "This idiot."

Nate gasped. "Oh."

Jamie sputtered, "I, um, she, we, uh."

Bo slapped his knee. "Well hell, that makes sense."

Jamie groaned, face in his hands.

Davis grinned into her stew. If declaring their togetherness did anything, it should make Jamie run the opposite direction.

The men settled close to the fire as the night cooled. Stories began. Hunting mishaps, mostly Nate's fault, near misses, embarrassing moments. Davis listened, elbow against Jamie's.

At one point, Nate nudged her. "Hey Davis, thanks for not yelling at us all day."

She smiled. "You're welcome."

Bo raised his cup. "To surviving day one."

Clay lifted his. "To stew better than my ex-wife's cooking and bread that should be illegal."

Jamie added, "To not dying tomorrow."

Davis froze. "Why would we die tomorrow?"

Jamie shrugged. "Good odds we won't."

"Jamie!"

He tried not to laugh. "I'm kidding. Mostly."

She shoved him lightly.

Night settled around them. And for the first time since they'd arrived, Davis felt a strange fondness toward the three hunters.

They were ridiculous.

But they weren't cruel. Okay, they were cruel to the animals, but not her.

Jamie

The next morning was quiet.

Fog drifted low, curling between tree trunks. Dew clung to the grass. Jamie crouched near the campsite, brows drawn tight, studying something.

Davis approached, rubbing sleep from her eyes. "What is it?"

He pointed.

Fresh prints.

Large and circular with claws.

Her stomach tightened. "Mountain lion?"

"Yeah."

She swallowed. "Close?"

"Close enough that I'm not thrilled," he admitted quietly. "Tracks cut right through our camp."

Bo, Clay, and Nate stumbled out of their tents.

Nate yawned. "Morning. What's the plan today?"

Jamie didn't answer immediately. Davis did.

"Staying alive."

Nate blinked. "Wait, why did you say it like that?"

Jamie stood. "Everyone stays behind me. Single file. No noise. Grab some energy bars."

The men nodded nervously, grabbed their weapons, and did as he said.

They hiked a narrow path along the ridge, fog clinging to their ankles. Jamie led, Davis directly behind him, the hunters in a tight line behind her.

It took all of ten minutes for Nate to complain.

"Do you feel like we're being watched?" he whispered.

"Yes," Davis whispered back.

"Nate," Bo hissed. "Stop talking."

But the forest seemed wrong somehow.

Too still.

Even the birds held their breath.

Jamie raised a hand for silence.

They all froze.

Jamie saw it then. A flicker of tan fur between two boulders. A tail. A flash of muscle coiled low.

His breath caught.

"Jamie," Davis whispered, "left."

He nodded once.

The lion stepped out, its golden eyes stayed unblinking. It was about six feet from Nate.

Nate made a noise that could best be described as "tiny dying squirrel."

The lion's gaze locked onto him.

Of course it did.

Nate was flailing, trying to move away.

Flailing was prey behavior.

Jamie whispered, "Stand still."

Nate whispered back, "I can't."

The lion moved a single step.

Davis moved two.

She stepped in front of Nate, spreading her arms wide, making herself look larger, more threatening, exactly what Jamie had drilled into her during the first hunt.

"Davis—" Jamie warned, too late.

She hissed sharply at the lion, stomping her boot in the dirt.

Surprisingly, lions did not expect angry vegan women defending panicked hunters.

The cat's head jerked back, clearly startled.

Bo whispered, "What the hell is Davis doing?!"

Clay whispered back, "Protecting Nate from himself."

Jamie stepped forward carefully, hands open.

"Easy, easy, no one moves."

Davis didn't break eye contact with the lion. "Jamie," she whispered, "he's scared."

"I know."

"Help him."

A moment of stillness.

The lion blinked.

Jamie slowly reached back and tapped Nate's arm. "Move behind Bo. Slowly."

Nate obeyed, shaking like a leaf.

Davis held her ground.

The lion's ears flicked. It exhaled, growled low, clearly annoyed, then turned and slipped back into the rocks. Totally soundless, regal, and uninterested.

Gone.

Davis exhaled hard, knees nearly buckling.

Jamie caught her arm. "Hey."

"I'm fine," she whispered, though her legs disagreed.

Nate threw his arms around her from behind. "You saved me!"

She stumbled under his weight. "Oh God, don't hug me, you're sweaty."

Bo whooped. "Holy hell, woman! You stared down a mountain lion!"

Clay shook his head in awe. "You've got guts."

Jamie looked at her with something different then turned to the men.

"Not one of you raised your weapons."

"You told us we were hunting elk."

He had but these idiots should have had the sense to protect themselves. He turned back to Davis and felt something different than he had before. Something like pride and fear and affection all tangled together.

He pulled her aside gently. "You could've been hurt."

"But I wasn't."

"You scared me."

She softened. "I wasn't letting Nate die."

Jamie looked toward Nate, who was pacing in a circle muttering, "I saw my life flash before my eyes," and sighed.

"Thank you," he said quietly.

"For what?"

"For proving I'm not the only one protecting them."

For a moment, neither of them spoke.

Davis finally smiled. "You're welcome, Calloway."

Chapter Twenty-Five

DAVIS

Back at the camp, Nate practically tackled her again.

"You saved my life," he gasped, voice shuddering with devotion. "My actual, entire life! I am reborn!"

He'd obviously been dwelling on his near-death experience. Davis peeled him off like a wet jacket. "Please stop sweating on me."

Bo grabbed her hand like she'd just won Miss America. "That was the bravest thing I've ever seen."

Clay nodded reverently. "Seriously. I'm pretty sure the lion feared you."

Nate slapped both hands to his cheeks. "Davis Bernard: Mountain Lion Slayer."

"She didn't slay anything," Jamie muttered.

But it didn't matter. Nate was already chanting it under his breath like a victory song.

"Mountain Lion Slayer, Mountain Lion Slayer."

Bo knelt suddenly.

On the ground.

In front of her.

"Your Majesty," he said gravely. "We are unworthy."

Davis blinked. "Please stand up. If anyone walks by, they'll think this is a cult."

Clay approached with his water bottle. "Do you need hydration, Slayer?"

"Not Slayer," Jamie snapped. "Davis. Her name is Davis."

Bo nodded solemnly. "Slayer Davis."

Jamie groaned.

Nate shoved a granola bar at her. "For strength."

Davis blinked. "I need strength?"

"Strength needs sustenance," Nate said dramatically.

She accepted the granola bar because refusal would probably cause him emotional distress. "Thank you."

Bo reached over and patted Nate proudly. "Our woman saved you."

Jamie's head whipped around so sharply she thought he might've sprained something.

"She's not—" Jamie began.

But Bo was already continuing. "This group has always needed strong feminine leadership."

"She's not our woman," Jamie insisted.

"Technically, she's *your* woman," Clay added unhelpfully, examining his nails.

Jamie choked. "She's not. Stop saying that."

"Do you deny your love?" Nate gasped dramatically.

Jamie sputtered in horror. "Davis, help me."

But Davis was doubled over laughing.

"What the hell is happening," Jamie muttered, glaring at her. "This is your fault."

She wiped tears from her eyes. "I'm sorry," she lied.

He glared harder. "You are not sorry."

"No," she admitted, still breathless. "Not at all."

The men clung to her like she was both protector and celebrity.

They went back out and it only got worse.

Bo carried her pack. Clay brushed twigs away from her path. Nate walked behind her in case she "needed a human shield."

It was ridiculous.

Hilarious.

And deeply inconvenient for Jamie's sanity.

Because for the rest of the day, his jaw worked overtime in silent frustration.

After hiking for three hours, they paused at a clearing for a break. Bo offered Davis the prime sitting spot on a fallen log. Clay handed her his best trail mix. Nate fanned her with a notebook.

Jamie watched from the side like a man who'd discovered a new, uncomfortable emotion and hated every second of it.

He stood with his arms crossed, eyes narrowed at the hunters, jaw tight enough to crack teeth.

Davis leaned back, smirking slightly. "You're glaring."

"I'm not glaring."

"You are definitely glaring."

"I'm observing."

"Observing angrily."

He exhaled sharply, running a frustrated hand through his hair. "They're ridiculous."

She grinned. "They're nice."

"They're worshipping you."

She shrugged. "I deserve it."

He dragged a hand down his face. "Davis. They could have easily shot that damned cat."

Nate suddenly sprinted toward her. "Slayer Davis! I found a better sitting rock!"

Jamie nearly tackled him. "Nate. She. Can. Sit. Wherever. She. Wants."

Nate blinked. "Are you mad at me?"

Jamie inhaled, nostrils flaring. "I'm not mad."

Clay whispered to Bo, "He's absolutely mad."

Bo whispered back, "He's in love."

Jamie's head snapped around. "I can hear you!"

Davis nearly fell off her log due to laughter.

Jamie's jealousy simmered all the way back to camp after an unfruitful day.

The hunters served Davis dinner.

Served.

Like waiters.

Bo brought her a steaming cup of cocoa.

Clay presented a perfectly carved stick to roast her tofu on. Nate shooed away imaginary bugs around her head.

Jamie stared into the fire; arms crossed like a sulking bear.

"You okay?" she asked softly, sitting beside him.

He didn't look at her. "Perfect."

"Liar."

He finally turned his head. His eyes flicked over her. They were frustrated and a little helpless.

"They won't leave you alone."

She nudged his knee with hers. "Maybe I like the attention."

He stiffened. "Do you?"

She leaned in, voice dropping. "Not as much as I like yours."

His breath stopped.

Just stopped.

Bo shouted suddenly, ruining the moment: "Slayer Davis! Would you like more cocoa?"

Jamie whirled around. "She's fine, Bo!"

Bo blinked. "Just being polite."

"Try being polite somewhere else."

Clay snorted. "Someone's jealous."

Jamie looked ready to throw him into the fire.

Davis rested her hand gently on Jamie's thigh under the cover of darkness, fingers brushing small circles.

He glanced down, startled.

She whispered, "Relax. They're harmless."

He swallowed, staring at her hand like he wasn't sure if he should move it or hold it.

"Davis."

"Hmm?"

"Don't do that unless you want me to—"

She raised an eyebrow. "To what?"

He shut his mouth hard, cheeks flushing in the firelight.

Bo plopped down beside them with a grin. "Man, you two are entertaining."

Jamie stood abruptly. "We're going to bed."

"We?" Bo echoed.

"We as in Davis and me," Jamie snapped. "Goodnight."

He grabbed Davis's hand and marched her away from the fire before she could embarrass him further.

She followed, laughing under her breath.

Chapter Twenty-Six

DAVIS

She woke to the sound of rustling outside the tent and three grown men arguing about protein bars.

Nate: "This says it expired in 2022."

Bo: "Expiration dates are suggestions."

Clay: "You're a suggestion."

She groaned and wiggled out of her sleeping bag just as Jamie zipped the tent open. He looked annoyingly handsome for someone who'd slept on a foam pad.

"Morning," he murmured, leaning in to kiss her cheek.

Her stomach fluttered. "Morning."

Outside, the hunters perked up immediately, as if she was a celebrity making a surprise appearance.

"Slayer Davis!" Nate exclaimed.

Jamie sighed. "Please stop calling her that."

Davis raised a hand. "Actually, I need to talk to you all."

Three grown men straightened like schoolboys caught chewing gum.

Jamie blinked. "Oh no."

Davis stepped to the center of camp and crossed her arms. "Sit."

Clay sat first. Nate practically collapsed. Bo hesitated until she raised an eyebrow, then lowered himself onto the log like he was awaiting sentencing.

Jamie muttered, "This is going to be good," and leaned against a tree to watch the carnage.

"Okay, gentlemen," Davis began. "We need to discuss the ethics of killing elk."

Bo winced.

Clay sighed.

Nate whispered, "Do we need snacks for this?"

She ignored him.

"You came out here hoping to take home a trophy. A head on a wall. A bragging picture."

The men exchanged guilty looks.

"But tell me this: Did that elk harm you?"

Bo shook his head.

Clay frowned. "Well, no."

"Does killing it make you a better provider?"

Silence.

"Does it improve your appearance? Make you popular? Help anyone, anywhere?"

The men started to look uncomfortable. Good.

She pressed on, gentler now. "Or does it just give you a picture and a story you could get without taking a life?"

Clay stared at his boots. "Damn."

Nate sniffed dramatically. "Are you giving us feelings?"

Davis softened. "We've had an amazing adventure. You've seen incredible wildlife. But maybe, just this once, you let something big and beautiful stay big and beautiful."

Bo rubbed his jaw. "I never thought of it like that."

"Me neither," Clay admitted.

Nate looked at her with wide, emotional eyes. "You're like a wilderness therapist."

Jamie coughed to hide a groan.

Davis pointed uphill. "Elk graze up that ridge in the mornings. If you want a trophy, take a photo. Not a body."

The men exchanged glances.

Bo nodded slowly. "All right. Let's do it."

Clay stood, slinging his pack. "Photos only."

Nate put a hand over his heart. "For the elk."

Jamie just shook his head.

They climbed the ridge quietly. Astonishingly so. Davis suspected they feared disappointing her more than missing the elk.

Jamie whispered, "You terrify them."

"I terrify you sometimes," she whispered back.

"You terrify me in different ways."

She grinned. "Good."

At the ridge crest, they spotted them. Three elk, two females and a large bull, standing in the soft morning light, their breath puffing in small clouds, antlers catching the sun.

Clay whispered, "Damn, it's beautiful."

Bo raised his phone reverently. "I suddenly don't want to shoot it."

Nate sniffled again. "We're witnessing a majestic moment in our lives."

Jamie glanced sideways at Davis, something odd flickering across his face. "I can't believe you managed this."

She blushed.

The hunters took dozens of pictures. Some were serious, some ridiculous. At one point, Nate posed like he was presenting a game show prize, whispering, "Behold: Elk."

The animals watched them for a long moment, unbothered, then trotted deeper into the forest. Unharmed. Alive.

Bo exhaled. "That was way better than a kill shot."

Clay nodded hard. "Absolutely."

Nate grinned. "I'm calling this my spiritual awakening."

Jamie rolled his eyes. "Don't overdo it."

Davis smiled. "I'm proud of you guys."

They beamed.

By the time they trekked back to the drop-off point the following day, the pilot's plane buzzed overhead, dipping its wings lazily before landing on the dusty strip.

Bo clapped Jamie on the back. "You're a good guide, Calloway."

"You too, kid," Jamie said, ruffling Nate's hair.

"I'm twenty-three," Nate muttered.

Then they turned to Davis.

Bo thrust out his hand. "Thank you. For everything."

Clay bowed. "Our queen."

Nate saluted her. "Slayer."

"I saved you from a lion. Don't waste this precious life," Davis told him dramatically.

"I'll live up to your expectations, promise," Nate said with feeling.

Jamie stepped beside her, his arm going around her shoulder. "Take care, guys."

Bo pointed at Jamie, smirking. "And you take care of her."

Jamie glared. "I, she, just get on the plane."

The hunters loaded up and waved out the small window as the plane rattled down the makeshift runway and lifted off.

Davis watched until they were a speck in the sky.

Jamie watched her.

When she finally turned to him, he smiled softly. "I'm not sure what to say."

She shrugged. "Something nice?"

"I'll do that when it comes to mind," he said.

A warm breeze swept between them, and Jamie reached for her hand.

She let him take it.

"Ready to go home?" he asked as their plane came in for its landing.

"Yeah," she said. "Let's go home."

Chapter Twenty-Seven

JAMIE

He had fallen in love his freshman year of college. Or at least he thought he had. Now he realized it hadn't been love so much as convenience wrapped in admiration. Someone who liked him without really knowing him. Someone who fit comfortably into college life. Someone who didn't challenge him. Someone who didn't turn everything upside down.

Davis Bernard did.

And damn it all, he'd completely lost the battle against himself. But he refused to call it love because it wasn't. Jamie Calloway didn't do love.

The last thing he wanted was to tie himself to a woman. His sisters had enough estrogen to last him a lifetime. He'd planned to stay single forever.

But something hit him on the plane ride back to the estate. It happened when she laughed at something he said, her head falling back slightly, sunlight catching in her hair. It hit him when she squeezed his hand after the hunters left. When she worked a leaf out of his hair. When she teased him about being jealous.

It hit him every time he caught her doing something unexpected, like feeding a squirrel trail mix or stopping to admire a mushroom colony like it was a modern art museum.

He was in lust with her. It was not love.

Fully. Stupidly. Irrevocably, in lust with her.

And he had no idea what to do to stop the other L word from encroaching.

He was a man who'd always lived on the move. He thrived on simplicity: gear, maps, long treks, quiet miles of untouched land. He liked a life without clutter. Without noise. Without emotional entanglements.

When all was said and done, he didn't make a lot of money. He barely afforded his one-bedroom apartment. And he liked it that way. Simple life, no one waiting for him, no one telling him what to do.

He'd taken Anthony Gables up on the will contingencies because it was an adventure. The fact that there might be money in it at the end of the year just made it better. He hadn't cared about the house. He definitely didn't care about the vegan he was forced to live with. And now he did. Cared about the old house too.

What the hell had happened? Settling down was something other people did. People who lived behind fences. People who liked routines and brunch menus and soft furniture.

People like Davis. She was everything he wasn't.

She loved people. Animals. Restaurants where waiters explained the ethical sourcing of tofu with reverence. She cared about animal rights, community gardens, sustainable living, political issues he barely followed. She listened to musicals at full volume while kneading dough. She wore color that didn't blend with her surroundings. She had opinions. Strong ones.

She was messy and vibrant and alive in ways he was not.

He felt deeply for her but it terrified him.

They would never work.

He scrubbed a hand over his face while imagining a future.

Her in his city apartment. Him in the wild. Her wanting a cozy home. Him restless without the mountains. Her fighting for causes. Him fighting the urge to keep her away from danger.

No overlap.

Except the way she looked at him sometimes, soft like she saw the man beneath all the wilderness and stubbornness.

Except the way she trusted him without question.

Except the way she fit against him when they slept, like she belonged there, like he'd been missing her shape all his life.

Except that he didn't want to imagine a future without her in it. He had to stop thinking about her. About them. Their fling needed to stay in the fling square.

She came out of the hall bathroom; her hair wrapped in a towel.

"You okay?" she asked.

He nodded.

Lie.

"You sure?" She adjusted the head towel. "You have a strange look on your face."

"I'm thinking."

"Uh-oh."

He huffed a laugh. "Not like that."

"Then like what?"

He hesitated.

She stepped closer. "Jamie."

The sound of his name in her voice. He almost told her everything right then.

"I just." He shook his head. "Nothing. Long hunt."

She studied him, her eyes searching his, softening slightly. She knew something was up. She knew him too well.

And that scared him too.

She hummed as she walked to her room.

He lusted for her.

Was lust enough to keep her around for a while? For a lifetime?

And why the hell did that thought encroach?

He only knew one thing for certain: He'd never wanted someone like this before. Never felt like this before.

Never been this afraid of losing something he didn't even have yet.

And he didn't know how to stop all the thoughts that jumbled inside his head.

Chapter Twenty-Eight

JAMIE

Jamie leaned back from his laptop, running both hands down his face as if doing so might erase the numbers on the screen. It didn't. They just stared rudely back at him.

He muttered a few words only raccoons and accountants should hear.

From the couch, Davis glanced up from her book. She was curled in a blanket like an adorable burrito. Exactly the kind of person who shouldn't witness his spiral.

"What's up?" she asked.

"Nothing," he lied.

She lowered her book. "Jamie."

He exhaled sharply. "My finances are not up, they're down."

She blinked. "Your finances?"

"Yes," he said flatly. "You know, the reason I work for a living? My love of food that costs money? Clothing, shoes, things that normal people buy without selling a kidney? Yeah. Those things."

Her brows pulled together. "Just like that, you're broke?"

The skepticism in her tone stung more than he expected. Late the previous year he broke his leg. His savings had the life sucked out of it and he was just beginning to recover. Well, until now. Until Davis and her abhorrence of killing things.

The inheritance, if there was money involved, would help him a lot but he knew he couldn't depend on it. It also sucked that he had to think about finances. He'd given up his apartment and hoped he would be able to build his savings during the year he lived in Anthony's house. That dream was coming to a sad end, that nomad lifestyle he loved might never be at his fingertips again.

He turned to face her fully. "I make good money as a guide. But most of that money comes in the form of tips, after the hunter bags the animal they're after."

She wrinkled her nose. "You use the word 'bag' like it's not death in that bag."

"I use the word 'bag' because that's what it's called," he said tiredly. "Did you miss the part about tips?"

"Oh," she murmured.

"Yeah," he added, voice flat. "Anthony and Trevor didn't tip me. Not a single dollar. That's never happened before."

Her lips parted in shock. "The boys didn't leave you a tip either?"

"The boys?" He narrowed his eyes. He knew damn well who she meant, but hearing her call the three hunters "the boys" fired every competitive instinct in his bloodstream.

She smirked. "My fan club."

He closed his eyes. Wonderful.

"Yes," he said, "they gave a tip. But it was only half of what they gave me last time."

Davis didn't look even remotely guilty. If anything, she looked proud.

"You should count on lower tips," she said breezily. "Think of the adventures you'll have with no animals dying." She gave a bright, obnoxiously sunshine-filled smile. "You're about to become a photographer's wet dream."

He covered his eyes with both hands. "You're not helping," he mumbled into his palms.

She didn't get it, of course she didn't. She didn't understand what it was like to survive off inconsistent seasonal income. She didn't understand that being a good guide meant guiding all kinds of hunters, even the ones you didn't morally agree with.

He took the jobs because someone would take them if he didn't. And he'd rather it be him, someone who respected the animals, than someone reckless.

A soft hand touched his shoulder. Jamie looked up into Davis's hazel eyes. They were warm and full of conviction that didn't bend for anything.

"I want to feel badly," she said gently. "I really do. But those animals don't deserve to die."

He swallowed hard.

A spark of mischief lit her face, "It's my turn to take you somewhere. And tonight is the night. I have it all planned."

"Should I ask questions?" he murmured.

"No," she said brightly. "Absolutely not."

"That doesn't sound reassuring."

"It's something dangerous though," she said, squeezing his shoulder. "It'll make your heart pump and get you out of the doldrums."

Who used words like *doldrums*? Davis did. His pulse spiked for reasons that had nothing to do with danger.

"What kind of dangerous?" he asked.

The grin she gave him could have powered a small city.

"Oh, Jamie," she said, giving a body stretch that shot heat straight down his spine, "you're going to love this."

He groaned into his hands again.

He wouldn't love it financially.

Nor rationally.

But God help him.

He was going to follow her anyway.

Chapter Twenty-Nine

JAMIE

He should have known something was wrong the moment Davis made him dress in all black. Not his usual dark hiking gear. No. Black jeans, black long-sleeved shirt, black beanie. Jamie looked like a bargain-bin cat burglar.

Meanwhile, Davis bounced around the entryway covering her hair with a black beanie like this was a hiking date.

"Why do we look like we're about to commit a felony?" he asked.

She gave him a blinding smile. "Because we are doing something brave."

"Brave usually means legal."

"In some places."

"In most places!"

She patted his cheek. "Don't worry, my friend arranged everything."

"That does not reassure me."

Her "friend" arrived ten minutes later. Shady, with purple hair, combat boots, and the energy of someone who got her coffee from an IV drip was almost more than he could take.

Jamie shook her hand. "So, what exactly are we doing tonight?"

Shady grinned like she'd been waiting for the question. "A liberation."

Jamie froze. "A what?"

Davis elbowed him excitedly. "A chicken liberation."

Shady nodded solemnly. "We're freeing the oppressed."

"Oh my God," Jamie whispered. "I'm going to jail."

Shady clapped him on the shoulder. "Relax. I used to be PETA and I know what I'm doing."

Jamie pinched the bridge of his nose. "PETA is a terrorist organization and the fact you were part of it does not make me feel better."

Shady's face reddened and she got a look in her eyes that made Jamie take a step back. "PETA may be controversial and it has been criticized for its rhetoric and undercover tactics, but it is not legally or officially classified as a terrorist organization in the U.S. or elsewhere. Have I made myself clear?"

The drive was long and quiet. The sky was dark. Too dark. Jamie didn't like the silence. He didn't like the backroads. He didn't like whatever "liberation" meant in Davis's vocabulary.

They pulled up to a chain-link fence behind a large industrial building. Lights hummed overhead. The smell hit him first. Sour. Bad. And simply wrong.

"This place raises chicks?" Jamie asked, stomach twisting.

Shady nodded. "Factory farm. The female babies are kept in crates. No sunlight. No room. No enrichment. The male chicks are put immediately into a grinder and used for feed."

Davis swallowed hard. "These babies can't even spread their wings, Jamie."

He looked at her then.

All fire, compassion, and rage she didn't know how to contain.

He was screwed. For so many reasons.

Shady pulled out a bolt cutter the size of Jamie's arm.

Jamie jerked back. "No. Absolutely—"

"Relax," she said, slicing through the padlock in one fluid motion. "They fired half their night staff. Nobody monitors this side."

"This is a crime," Jamie whispered.

"This is justice," Davis whispered back, eyes blazing.

They stepped inside the fence and made their way to a long white building. Shady popped that lock too. They stepped inside.

Jamie had seen horrible things in the wild. Injured animals, abandoned pets, starving wildlife. But nothing prepared him for rows of crates stacked like filing cabinets, filled with tiny yellow chicks.

They chirped weakly, crowded together, barely able to move. Many had missing feathers. Some were trembling.

Jamie's chest tightened painfully. "Holy hell."

Davis's eyes filled with tears. "This is what they call humane. Notice that many have missing feet because the wire flooring shreds into them."

Shady cracked her knuckles. "All right, troops. Front crates first. Open, gather, relocate. Keep them warm against your chest."

"Relocate to where?" Jamie asked.

"The crates I brought for now and then my cousin's sanctuary," Shady said. "He specializes in rescued farm animals."

Jamie blinked. "In illegal chickens?"

"Focus, Calloway," Davis said. She was already at the first crate, easing it open with gentle hands. "Come here, sweetheart."

The chick nuzzled her neck immediately.

Jamie felt something twist inside him.

These chicks were no longer future nuggets with a side of ketchup, they were babies.

"Okay," he said softly. "Tell me what to do."

Davis looked at him, relief and gratitude filling her entire face. "Help me save as many as possible."

And he did.

He opened crates, scooping up fragile, trembling little bodies with careful hands. They chirped loudly, clinging to his shirt, tiny feet scratching against his chest.

Shady packed carriers in the van outside, moving like a chaotic superhero.

Davis worked beside him, focused, angry, and tender. Every time she whispered to a chick, it sounded like a promise.

Jamie found his throat tightening. "This is a lot of suffering."

"It's awful," she said. "But we can fix a little of it. Just this small part."

They moved row by row.

By the time they filled the last carrier, Jamie carried a chick who refused to leave him.

Shady glanced back into the building. "I have a large cardboard box left. We can take ten more without suspicion."

Davis nodded.

Jamie looked down at the chick perched in his palm, its tiny beak tapping his thumb.

It was shivering.

That was it. His heart snapped into a million pieces.

He cupped the yellow body gently to his chest. "You're coming too," he told the tiny critter.

Shady grinned. "Hell yes."

They loaded the chicks carefully into the van. Jamie kept the one pressed to his shoulder.

They rattled down the dark backroad, stacked with carriers full of softly peeping chicks. Jamie sat wedged between two crates, his chosen rescue tucked against his collar like a fuzzy, fragile caterpillar.

Davis sat across from him, watching with a soft smile that made him feel things he had no business feeling while covered in down feathers.

"You okay over there?" she asked, her voice warm in the dim glow of the dashboard lights.

"Fine," Jamie murmured, stroking the tiny chick's back with one cautious finger. "He likes my neck."

Davis grinned. "You're her emotional support human now."

Shady snorted from the driver's seat. "Seems accurate."

Jamie rolled his eyes, but gently, because the chick shifted, settling more comfortably against his throat. Then it made another tiny, adorable chirping sound.

Followed by a tiny, not adorable sensation.

Warmth. Suspiciously warm. Right beneath his jaw.

Jamie froze. "Oh no."

Davis leaned forward. "What? What's wrong?"

He didn't move. "He, uh."

It chirped again.

Something slid down inside Jamie's shirt.

"Oh my God," he said, voice strangled. "He pooped on me."

Davis's eyes widened. "Where!?"

Jamie tugged his collar open and peeked inside. "Everywhere! All over, oh, that's warm. Why is it warm?"

Shady lost all composure and slapped the steering wheel. "Ha!"

Davis covered her mouth, shoulders shaking. "Jamie, don't panic."

"I'm not panicking," he said, absolutely panicking. "It's crawling. No, it's sliding. It's sliding down!"

He twisted, trying not to jostle the chick, but also desperately trying to dislodge the creeping warmth working its way toward his waistband.

Davis burst out laughing. Real, helpless laughter with tears pooling in her eyes.

"Jamie, stop moving! You're making it worse!"

"That's because it is worse," he hissed, shaking his shirt out. "How does something the size of a lemon produce this much, nope, not thinking about it."

Shady laughed so hard the van swerved.

Davis scooted over and gently retrieved the chick, holding it in her palms. "You poor thing."

Jamie pointed at her. "Are you talking to him or me?"

"Both, but it's a her. They kill all the males in the grinder, just toss the babies in and let them grind."

That caused Jamie to go silent for a moment.

She pulled a few tissues from her pocket because of course she had tissues, and patted his neck and chest like she was dusting a mantel. He sat there stiffly while she cleaned him up, cheeks burning hotter than the chicken poop.

Davis whispered, still smiling, "You're officially a chicken daddy now."

Jamie dropped his head back against the crate with a groan. "This is the worst night of my life."

Davis softly kissed his cheek. "No," she murmured. "It's one of your best."

She stared at him like he'd just lifted a car with one hand. "You're a natural," she whispered. "Natural at chicken liberation and a natural at chicken daddyhood."

He snorted softly. "Don't say that. I'm trying not to get attached."

He took the chick back and tucked it into his neck again.

"You already named him didn't you," she accused.

"I did not," he insisted but even he knew it was a lie.

"What's his name?"

"Clovis," he muttered.

Shady cackled. "That is the most rugged cowboy chicken name I've ever heard."

Jamie sighed. "I hate both of you."

But he didn't.

Not even a little.

Davis touched his shoulder. "Thank you."

"For what?" he asked.

"For caring," she said softly.

He didn't answer.

He was too busy realizing just how much he cared.

Chapter Thirty

JAMIE

A month had passed since the chicken caper, and Jamie still couldn't believe he'd participated in a poultry heist. Even worse? He'd apparently become the adoptive father of a bird with commitment issues.

Clovis was no longer the tiny ball of sunshine from the night of liberation. The chick was slowly morphing into something awkward. Straggly feathers sprouted at weird angles. Her legs were too big for her body and she had the attitude of a hungover pigeon.

And she had absolutely, unequivocally claimed him as her savior and his office as sovereign territory.

Davis insisted hens didn't have territories.

Jamie disagreed.

His chicken had rights, and if she wanted an office, then she damn well had an office.

Clovis currently slept in his lap as he worked on his laptop, a warm fuzzy paperweight. Jamie finished his email, closed the laptop as gently as a bomb technician diffusing a mine, and it made no difference.

The chick popped awake instantly, peeping indignantly.

"Well," Jamie sighed, "I guess that's my cue, princess."

He carried Clovis outside to the twelve-by-six-foot dog kennel he'd purchased with his own dwindling funds and converted into a tiny chicken palace. Shade hut, roosting bar, pine shavings and all. Davis called it ridiculous. Jamie called it responsible parenting.

He set Clovis down inside, tossed out a handful of feed, closed the latch, and turned toward the house just as a silver sedan rolled up the long gravel drive.

Jamie straightened, wiping dust off his jeans.

A middle-aged man stepped out, all polished shoes, silver hair, and the stiff posture of someone who never allowed himself to sweat in public. He carried a briefcase like it contained state secrets.

"Hello," the man said, waving politely as he approached. "I'm Peter Gilbrick. I was Mr. Gables's attorney."

Jamie shook his hand. "How can I help you?"

"I came to deliver a letter left by Mr. Gables." Gilbrick paused. "Actually, three letters. But I have strict instructions regarding when each can be delivered."

This man radiated confidentiality so hard Jamie almost saluted him.

"Come inside," Jamie offered. "Davis should hear this too."

Inside, Davis stood by the foyer, brows raised. She shook the attorney's hand firmly.

"It's about time," she said. "I have a lot of questions."

Gilbrick lifted both palms, expression regretful. "Unfortunately, I can't answer any of them. I'm only here to deliver what your uncle left for you."

He set his briefcase on the entryway table, clicked it open, and withdrew a plain manila envelope. No secretive markings. No return address. Just *Davis* written in Anthony Gables's distinctive slanted script.

Davis's hand trembled slightly as she took it. Her uncertain gaze shot to Jamie's.

Gilbrick cleared his throat. "Well. I'll be on my way."

"You must stay for tea. Or coffee," Davis insisted.

Gilbrick backed toward the door like hospitality was a trap. "Thank you, but I really must decline. I have another stop and a wife who expects me home for dinner."

He left quickly. Almost too quickly.

Jamie and Davis stood side by side, watching the sedan disappear down the drive.

"Did he seem nervous to you?" Jamie asked.

"He seemed weird," Davis muttered. "But everything about my uncle, this house, and now his lawyer is weird. Hopefully this," she held up the envelope, "finally gives us answers."

Jamie wasn't sure it would.

But he hoped, for her sake, that it did.

My Dearest Davis,

If you're reading this, it means you have been living in my home for at least three months without burning it down, selling it, or fleeing to the nearest vegan commune. Good. That means you stayed.

And if you stayed then you've begun to understand why I designed my will the way I did.

You were always too much for the small boxes people tried to place you in. Too opinionated. Too compassionate. Too unwilling to look away when something was wrong.

I loved that about you. But I worried for you, too.

This world is cruel.

You are soft in all the places that matter.

So I created the conditions to bring you to a place where softness could become strength and where strength could be softened.

You are not meant to live your life surrounded only by people who think as you do. You are meant to challenge and be challenged. I wanted you to live beside someone who would oppose you at every turn and still stand beside you anyway.

Enter Jamie Calloway.

No, you weren't chosen at random.

And yes, I knew exactly what I was doing.

Jamie is stubborn enough to hold his ground but kind enough to move it when he's wrong. He understands the land in a way most people never will. And I suspected that if you two were ever forced to depend on one another, you would learn something neither of you would learn alone.

Maybe you'll hate him.

Maybe you'll love him.

Maybe you'll do both on the same day.

Either way, you'll grow.

There are two more letters.

One is for Jamie.

The last is for you both.

Gilbrick knows when to deliver them. Trust him.

And Davis, whatever else happens in that house, please remember:

Not all cages have bars. Not all freedom looks like escape.

Live well.

Be brave.

And please, for the love of my old bones, don't turn my greenhouse into an animal pen.

With all my affection,

Uncle Theo

Chapter Thirty-One

JAMIE

Jamie did not consider himself an easily rattled man.

He'd survived blizzards, rockslides, angry hunters, campsites invaded by raccoons, one furious moose, and, most terrifying of all, a chicken who now believed his office was a sovereign nation.

But listening as Davis read her uncle's letter aloud?

That rattled him.

She stood in the living room with the envelope in one hand and the pages trembling in the other. Her eyes scanned line after line as she spoke, her expression shifting too quickly for him to keep up.

Sadness.

Surprise.

Annoyance.

Softness.

Confusion.

And something else. Something he couldn't name because it squeezed too tight around his ribs.

When she finally lowered the pages, she didn't speak. She just stood there breathing, like she wasn't sure how.

"Davis?" Jamie asked carefully. "You okay?"

She swallowed. "I don't know."

He stepped closer. "Do you want to talk about it?"

She let out a laugh. "He planned this. He actually planned it. He picked you. He thought we'd, I don't know, fix each other like some kind of cosmic therapy experiment."

Jamie nodded, even though his muscles had gone suddenly tight. "Yeah. I gathered that part."

She sat on the sofa, letter crumpling in her lap as she leaned forward, elbows on her knees. "Why didn't he just tell me what he wanted while he was alive? I never even knew him and had no idea he knew me. Why wait until after he died?"

Jamie eased onto the couch beside her. "Maybe because you wouldn't have done it."

She looked up. "You think I wouldn't have lived here?"

"I think," he said gently, "you'd have refused anything that looked like manipulation. You didn't know him."

Davis's mouth twisted. "This was manipulation."

"Sure," Jamie agreed. "But maybe not the cruel kind."

She exhaled hard. "He thought you would challenge me. How did he know anything about me? And he thought we'd be good for each other. That we'd—" She shook her head. "God. He expected too much and he's wrong?"

Jamie swallowed, because his heart was being ground to a pulp.

"What if he was right?" he asked softly. He had to.

Her gaze flicked toward him but moved quickly away. "I'm angry at him," she admitted. "And confused. And a little scared, I guess."

Jamie didn't move, afraid that if he did, he'd touch her. Pull her close. Say something he knew now that he couldn't say.

"You're scared?" he asked.

"Yes." She rubbed her forehead. "Because he knew me too well. And he knew you too."

Jamie let out a slow breath. "Can I tell you what it says to me?"

She nodded.

"It says that even without knowing us, he trusted us."

Her throat worked. Her fingers tightened on the letter. "Trusted us with what?"

"Each other," Jamie said honestly. "Maybe he thought we'd balance each other. Or grow. Or," he hesitated. "Or maybe he saw something we weren't ready to see yet."

Davis shut her eyes.

Jamie watched every breath she took, every tremble in her fingers. He wanted to reach out so badly his chest ached with it. To take her hand. Touch her shoulder. Something.

But he waited.

"Jamie," she whispered, "what if this changes everything?"

He swallowed. "Does it change how you feel?"

Her eyes opened slowly, meeting his. "I don't know yet."

Something in his chest twisted. He nodded. "That's okay."

"You're not upset?"

"I'm terrified," he said quietly, surprising even himself. "But I'm not upset."

Her breath hitched. "Why terrified?"

Because I love you.

The words lodged in his throat. They were too big, too dangerous, and too unrequited.

Instead, he said, "Because I don't want you to feel forced into something. Or pushed. Or manipulated by your uncle, or the house, or this situation. Or by me."

Her eyes softened then, just barely. "You're not pushing me."

"No?" he asked.

"No," she whispered. "If anything, you're holding back."

He let out a shaky breath, a half-laugh, half-exhale. "Yeah. Well. I'm trying not to screw this up."

A long silence stretched between them like a weighted blanket that offered comfort.

Finally, she placed the letter back in the envelope and held it to her chest.

"Jamie?"

"Yeah?"

"I think I need some time to think."

He nodded. "I can give you that." He didn't want to. He wanted to yell to the universe that this was unfair.

She stood slowly and stepped toward the hallway. Halfway there, she paused and glanced back at him.

"Thank you," she said softly. "For being you."

He smiled. "Always."

She disappeared down the hall.

Jamie sat there long after the sound of her feet disappeared.

He leaned back, covered his face with both hands, and let
himself finally feel the full weight of life.

The letter.

Her doubt.

His fear.

His love.

And the quiet, impossible truth gnawing at him: He
wasn't sure how to live without her anymore and she wasn't
sure how to live with him.

But he'd wait.

As long as she needed.

Because love wasn't the problem on his end. Davis's heart
was.

Chapter Thirty-Two

JAMIE

Giving Davis space proved harder than Jamie thought it would. He totally respected her request. But.

He emerged from his room early the following morning, dressed and focused on his mission: Distance.

He would let Davis breathe. Let her process. Let her feel out her emotions without him hovering like some love-struck, overly attached golden retriever.

He tiptoed past her closed door and whispered to himself, "Good. She's resting. I won't bother her."

Then he tripped over Clovis.

The chicken squawked. Loudly.

A beat later, Davis cracked open her bedroom door, eyes bleary from sleep. She blinked at him, her hair a sleepy red halo.

Jamie froze like a criminal caught mid-act.

"Why are you whispering?" Davis asked.

"I'm not whispering. Just, walking." He gestured vaguely. "Normal walking."

"You woke me."

"That was Clovis's fault."

Her gaze drifted to the chicken pecking his shoelace.

"Uh huh."

He cleared his throat. "I'll just go make coffee."

"That's my job," she said, frowning a little.

He panicked. "No! I mean, you take your time. I'll be out of your way."

"Okay," she murmured, confused.

He retreated so fast he inhaled his own breath.

The entire day went that way. Davis looked at him like he had a screw loose, and he felt out of place.

The next morning, he heard Davis in the kitchen at breakfast time, singing softly under her breath as she cooked. Normally, he would enter, steal a piece of sourdough, wrap his arms around her waist, and kiss her neck.

But today?

Nope. He was giving her space. It made for lonely nights but it was a sacrifice he had to make. So he waited in the hallway.

And he could smell sourdough.

And hear her humming.

And picture her doing that thing where she pushed her hair behind her ear.

He took two steps toward the kitchen then forced himself to step back.

Then forward again.

Then back.

He looked like he was doing an interpretive dance about indecision.

Finally, he backed away entirely. He'd eat cereal in his office. Alone. Sad. Like a man enduring self-inflicted punishment.

He poured cereal. Added oat milk from the small refrigerator he'd stocked, and sat.

A minute later, Davis appeared in the doorway holding a plate.

"Are you avoiding me?"

He jolted so hard the spoon flipped out of the bowl.

"Avoiding? No. Me? No. I'm just busy. With work. Very busy."

She studied him.

He stared at the wall behind her like it contained meaningful wisdom.

"I made you breakfast," she said quietly.

His heart twisted so sharply it nearly made a sound.

"Thank you," he said softly. "I'm just trying to give you the space you asked for," he finally admitted.

"I didn't ask for space," she corrected gently. "I asked for time."

"Oh."

"Those are two different things, Jamie."

He blinked. "Right. Yes. Absolutely. Of course."

But then she left the plate on the corner of his desk and walked out.

He didn't know if he should follow or stay or spontaneously combust.

He stayed.

He told himself she needed breathing room even if she wanted to call it time. That her uncle's letter was still processing and she deserved clarity without him muddying the waters.

So, he went outside to work on the shed. Hammering. Fixing shelves. Menial tasks that should've kept him occupied.

But every few minutes his brain whispered: *What is she thinking?*

Is she okay?

Could she love me?

Is she deciding she wants a life without me?

By hour five he was imagining scenarios involving her packing, leaving, moving back to the city. He imagined the house quiet. Empty. Her absence in every room like a ghost.

He imagined losing her.

And that was it.

He dropped the hammer.

He stomped toward the house, absolutely done with pretending he was unaffected.

He walked into the dining room just as Davis walked out of the kitchen holding a bowl of something warm and fragrant.

They both stopped.

Jamie inhaled deeply. "Okay, that's it. I can't do this."

Her eyebrows jumped. "Do what?"

"This! Time. Distance. Whatever the hell I've been doing."

He ran a hand through his hair, pacing once before turning to her. "I keep thinking I'm giving you time," he said, his breath uneven. "But all I'm doing is missing you. Constantly. And worrying I'm going to lose you if I say the wrong thing or breathe wrong or look at you too long."

Davis blinked and looked stunned.

"I heard you singing earlier," he confessed. "And I stood in the hallway like an idiot for ten minutes because I didn't know if walking into the kitchen counted as emotional pressure."

Her lips twitched. "Jamie."

"And then I ate cereal in my office like a lonely widower from a sad documentary."

She covered her mouth, laughing softly.

"And I just imagined you packing and leaving me and I realized I can't do this anymore." He stepped closer, heart pounding. "I don't want space from you. Not even a little bit."

Davis lowered the bowl slowly, her gaze softening. "Jamie," she whispered, "I didn't want space from you either."

He froze. "You didn't?"

"No," she said. "I just needed time to think. You're not the problem. My uncle is the problem. The situation is the problem. Not you."

He exhaled, more like a collapse than breath. "Okay. Good. Because I'm terrible at space."

"Yeah," she said, stepping closer, "you really are."

"Maybe the worst."

"Probably."

"And I'm not going to get better."

"I hope not," she said.

He swallowed, emotion thick in his chest. "So, what do we do now?"

She reached up and slid her fingers into his.

"We figure it out together," she said softly. "But you don't have to disappear to make room for me."

He leaned his forehead against hers and allowed the relief to wash through him. "Thank God," he murmured. "Because I'm better when you're here."

Her breath caught.

And finally, he allowed himself to touch her, pulling her into his arms with a soft, shaky exhale.

This time she didn't hesitate.

She melted into him like she'd been waiting.

And Jamie realized that giving her space had never been the answer.

Being close was.

Chapter Thirty-Three

JAMIE

Three days after their awkward-but-perfect reunion, life settled into a rhythm that was dangerously close to domestic.

Davis baked in the mornings, always barefoot, always humming. Jamie took Clovis out for "morning, afternoon, and evening constitutional time," proudly pretending it wasn't ridiculous. And they bumped into each other in the kitchen too often to be accidental, brushed hands too often to be innocent, and smiled too often not to be in trouble. Not to mention the nights, which were mind blowing.

Exciting.

Comfortable.

Easy.

Exactly the sort of thing the universe hated because on Wednesday afternoon, comfort died a quick death.

Jamie was in the yard repairing a loose patio board when an unmarked white car rumbled up the driveway. The sort of car that looked like it delivered bad news, subpoenas, or meat from its trunk.

The driver stepped out with a wrinkled white dress shirt and a clipboard in hand.

"Afternoon," he called. "You Jamie Calloway?"

Jamie wiped his hands on his jeans. "Yeah. Who are you?"

The man didn't answer. He went straight to the trunk, lifted out a large brown box, and carried it over.

"I was instructed to deliver this today." He thrust it into Jamie's stunned arms.

"What is it?" Jamie asked.

"No idea. My job is to deliver it." The man shoved the clipboard at him. "Sign where it's highlighted."

Two names were highlighted: Jamie Calloway and Davis Bernard.

Jamie frowned. "Let me grab Davis so she can sign too—"

"No need," the man interrupted quickly. "Either signature works."

"Who told you that?"

The man's entire body language shifted and his eyes darted around, foot tapping, someone deeply uncomfortable with being asked to think. "Well, I'm, uh, not sure I'm supposed to say."

Jamie's suspicion flared.

Before he could press further, Davis stepped onto the porch, wiping flour off her hands, eyes bright.

Until she saw Jamie's face.

"What's going on?" she called.

The deliveryman panicked, snatched the clipboard back, and practically sprinted for his car. "Thank you, sir. Have a good day!"

He peeled out so fast he nearly took down the mailbox at the end of the drive.

Davis hurried down the steps. "Jamie, what is it?"

He pointed at the box resting at his feet. "A gift. Or maybe a bomb."

"A bomb?"

"I'm sure it isn't a bomb," he said. "But I'm tired of surprises. First your uncle's will, then the letters, now this. I want answers."

"Well," she said, hands going to her hips, "if you're sure it isn't a bomb, let's take it inside and open it."

"It could still be a bomb."

She rolled her eyes. "You are suddenly very pessimistic."

"I've always been pessimistic. You just didn't notice until now."

She disarmed him entirely by rising on her toes and kissing his cheek. "Then I'll be the optimist. We make the perfect team."

He was defenseless.

Jamie picked up the box and followed her inside. They headed straight for the dining room.

"I'll get scissors," she said.

He pulled out a pocketknife. "You underestimate me."

Davis eyed the blade. "You carry that around the house?"

"I do man stuff around the house," he said, flicking it open. "Of course I carry a knife. This barely counts as one anyway."

She sniffed dramatically. "You arc such a—," her face twisted in mock disgust, "hunter."

He pretended not to hear her and sliced the tape.

Davis reached inside first, pulling out layers of brown crumpled packing paper.

Then she lifted something out.

A wooden box.

Heavy, carved, expensive looking. And locked.

Jamie whistled softly. "Fancy."

"Not helpful," Davis muttered, shaking it. "It's locked."

She dug through the packing paper for a key.

"Check for a note that explains what the hell this is about," Jamie said.

Nothing.

"Who was that guy?" she asked.

"No clue. And he wouldn't answer my questions."

"Did you get a copy of what you signed?"

Jamie stared at her. "You watched me sign it. You know I didn't."

She smiled. "Just checking."

They examined the wooden box again.

"It needs one of those old barrel keys," Davis said. "This is turning into a bad mystery."

Jamie snorted. "Does a good mystery exist?"

She shrugged. "We need the key. It has to be in the house."

"Why would it be in the house?"

"Think about it. Mysterious will. Mysterious attorney. Mysterious delivery guy. Mysterious box. Where else would the key be?"

Annoyingly, it made sense.

Thus began the Great Key Hunt.

Kitchen drawers. Bedroom closets. The study floorboards. Jamie found dust bunnies so large Clovis could've ridden one like a horse.

No key.

Davis rifled through her uncle's desk, muttering. "Check behind the books."

Jamie pulled back a row on the top shelf. A spider scurried out. He nearly launched the entire shelf across the room and may have made a noise that sounded similar to a scream.

Davis doubled over laughing. "So brave. So manly. I can't believe you don't like spiders."

"I've never liked them. Actually prefer roaches. Spiders are unpredictable and they're not even insects. Think scorpions, ticks, mites, whip scorpions, pseudoscorpions. They all have eight legs. Insects have six legs like they should. That spider had murder in its eyes."

"Was it carrying a key?"

"No key."

They regrouped even though Jamie knew she was laughing at him. Frustrated. Sweaty. Spider-traumatized, they continued the hunt.

An hour passed.

"I'm calling Gilbrick," Jamie said, pulling out his phone.

One ring. Two. Three.

Voicemail.

"Try again," Davis whispered.

He did.

Voice-freaking-mail.

He tried a third time. And a fourth.

Nothing.

"He's avoiding us," Davis said, pacing.

"Most likely," Jamie muttered. "This has to be connected to your uncle's letters."

"What now?" she asked.

"We check the attic."

Jamie grimaced. "The attic has its own spider ecosystem."

"Clovis could handle it."

"Clovis is a baby."

"She pooped on you like a champion spider control system."

Jamie sighed. "Fine. Attic."

The attic looked exactly like a place secrets went to die. Dust thick enough to sculpt and spiderwebs in every corner. Old trunks. Boxes that probably contained junk. Clovis began pecking everywhere she could reach.

They dug. And dug.

Photos. Receipts from the 80s. A collection of spoons from restaurants that had probably closed a decade ago. One wooden duck so hideous it should've been a crime.

But no key.

Davis sat back on her heels, frustrated. "It has to be somewhere. Why would he send a locked box without a key?"

Jamie wiped his brow. "What if he didn't send it?"

She looked at him. "What are you saying?"

"What if this has nothing to do with the house?"

Davis shook her head. "Right. You said the page you signed had both our names. Our names are only connected by this house."

They froze.

Jamie darted to the attic window and moved the curtain aside.

A sleek black SUV pulled up the drive.

Not the white car. Not familiar.

But the man who stepped out was.

"Gilbrick," Jamie breathed.

He looked shaken. Sweaty. Out of breath. And holding a thick manila envelope like it contained nuclear codes.

They scrambled down the attic ladder, nearly tripping, and met the lawyer at the front door.

"Mr. Gilbrick?" Davis gasped. "We've been calling you!"

Gilbrick looked around like he feared being watched. "I know. I came as soon as I could."

Jamie folded his arms. "What's going on?"

Gilbrick handed over the sealed envelope. "This letter wasn't supposed to be delivered until six months after you moved in. But my intern, the idiot that he is, delivered a box you were not meant to receive yet."

Davis blinked. "You mean the box with no key?"

"Yes." Gilbrick looked like he might faint. "This is extremely out of order."

Jamie squished the envelope corners aggressively.

Gilbrick stared at him in horror. "What are you doing?"

"Looking for a key," Jamie deadpanned.

Gilbrick closed his eyes, and rubbed his forehead. "For the love of," he stopped. "Just read the letter. It will clarify things."

Then he practically sprinted to his SUV and sped off.

Davis stood frozen, envelope in hand.

Jamie rested a hand on her back. "You want to open it here?"

She swallowed. "Not yet. There's one more place I want to check." She hesitated, looking at him. "The letter is yours. You should open it."

"I'm afraid it will bite."

Chapter Thirty-Four

DAVIS

The greenhouse was the one place they hadn't searched, mostly because Davis worked in it each day and hadn't noticed a key. But her uncle's previous letter had hinted, cryptically, of course, that he'd loved the greenhouse. That alone made Davis suspicious.

She pushed open the warped wooden door. Hinges groaned as sunlight filtered through dusty glass panels, spilling long, soft beams across the room. The smell of earth and damp leaves mingled with the faint sweetness of potting soil and she was in heaven. Add in the growing vines that climbed lazily up the corners, trying their best to escape through the roof and she was ready to toss a mattress inside and use the place as her bedroom.

She had a feeling that if her uncle had hidden anything, this was exactly the kind of dramatic location he'd choose.

The potting bench had its own space. Davis moved toward it slowly, her breath caught somewhere between hope and dread.

Jamie walked beside her, scanning the area with the hyper-focus of a man looking for traps, treasure, or spiders, possibly all three.

He saw it first.

"Davis." His voice dropped.

He pointed to something near the bench leg. A metal hinge, half-buried under dust and peeling paint, so faint it looked like an organic part of the bench.

Her pulse leapt.

She knelt, brushed away the dust, and revealed a wooden panel cleverly embedded into the bench itself.

A hidden compartment.

Of course, her uncle would hide something in a greenhouse. The man probably thought he was starring in his own mystery dinner theater.

Her breath hitched. "Please let this be the key."

Jamie crouched beside her. "Only one way to find out."

Together, they lifted the panel. The wood creaked open, releasing a puff of stale air. Inside sat a matchbox and a folded note taped to the lid.

Davis's stomach twisted when she recognized the handwriting. Her uncle's.

She peeled the note off and read:

If you're reading this, I'm dead.

"That's it?" She stared at the box as if it might explode. "Why would he write it like that?"

Jamie rested a warm, steady hand over hers. "Because your uncle had a flair for the dramatic."

"That's not comforting."

"I'm trying."

Despite the questions curling in her chest, she gave him a tiny, fleeting smile.

Carefully, she opened the box.

Inside a single key gleamed softly in the filtered sunlight. She held it up between them. "The carved box or the letter first?"

Jamie scratched the back of his neck. "I think, uh, the letter?"

"You think?" she echoed incredulously.

His stomach growled like a small bear.

He shrugged sheepishly. "I'm starving."

She stared at him. "Seriously?"

"I have a tapeworm," he said solemnly. "Or a very active metabolism."

"You just inhaled two breakfast sandwiches before we came out here!"

"Sandwiches are snacks."

She threw her hands up. "Fine. Food first, mystery later."

Back inside, Davis placed vegan cheese and crackers on a wooden serving board. She refused, on principle, to call it a charcuterie board. Charcuterie involved cured meats. This board was vegan and displayed only cheese and crackers. Morally superior cheese and crackers. Cheese and crackers that harmed not one animal.

Jamie scarfed down every bite like a man who hadn't eaten since the Jurassic period.

"Hungry much?" she asked as he licked a smear of nut-based brie off his thumb.

"You're a damned fine cook," he said through a mouthful, "but vegan food isn't filling."

She crossed her arms and looked him up and down. "You've been here months. I doubt you've lost a single ounce."

"Shoot me," he said, hands raised in surrender. "I like food. I'm always hungry. Are you going to sit there judging me or join in?"

"I'll watch."

"Creepy," he muttered affectionately.

After he finished, she cleared the board and sat beside him at the table. His fingers curled around the envelope with his name written across the front.

Jamie blew out a quiet breath. "All right. Here goes nothing."

He tore the letter open and unfolded the pages. He read aloud.

Jamie,

I know you and Davis feel as if you've been played. Maybe you have. This feisty old man is haunting you from the grave. Believe it! And don't underestimate your grandfather. That ornery old cuss will most definitely haunt you in this house.

Or maybe these two old men are trying to right a long-ago wrong.

A box will be delivered tomorrow. It will provide most of the answers you seek.

The key to the box is in the greenhouse. I'll let you do a scavenger hunt to find it because I know between you and Davis it won't be hard.

Jamie stopped reading.

Davis stared at the carved wooden box. Locked, waiting, and they had the key.

"Jamie," she whispered. "Whatever is inside that box it holds answers."

Jamie reached for her hand under the table. "I'm ready for answers."

Chapter Thirty-Five

DAVIS

They stood over the box like two archaeologists about to uncover the lost city of Why-Did-My-Family-ly-Keep-So-Many-Secrets, and with twin breaths of anticipation, lifted the lid.

Inside, envelopes. They sat in perfectly organized rows. It looked less like family correspondence and more like someone had been preparing a time-capsule-themed PowerPoint presentation for old people.

Jamie blinked at the stack. "Your uncle never claimed the truth would be quick," he muttered, taking in the sheer mountain of paper. "This is years' worth of writing. Maybe decades. Possibly centuries."

"How many do you think are here?" Davis asked, poking the top envelope like it might multiply.

"One hundred. Maybe two." He made a sweeping gesture. "Or seven thousand. Honestly, I lost count after twenty."

"No time like the present." She squared her shoulders. "There's a reason they're in order. We read them from start to finish, together."

"I'd rather go hunt for food or something," he said, sounding hopeful, like maybe she'd hand him a rifle and call it enrichment time at the zoo.

Davis slowly turned her head and gave him the kind of glare villains reserve for the moment they reveal their evil plan. "Our food needs to be harvested, not hunted. I brought a wild herb book with me, and if you're nice, I'll lend it to you. Your pocketknife should be the only weapon you need."

He blinked. "Haha. You're funny."

She widened her eyes innocently. "I'm sorry, big hunter man. I forgot you don't like reading. It might damage your alpha image."

"I just prefer activities that don't involve letters." He waved at the box like it had personally insulted him. "And tiny handwriting. And feelings."

"What if," she suggested sweetly, "I read them aloud, and you point out interesting facts. I'll even let you point out the macho facts."

"That shouldn't suck as badly," he admitted.

She shook her head. "You are such a baby. A very large baby with a beard."

He didn't deny it.

After fetching herself tea and Jamie his coffee, he claimed caffeine made him tolerate reading better, though she suspected it just made him louder, she settled cross-legged on the rug, where they moved the box. She pulled out the first letter.

Davis cleared her throat grandly. "Letter one."

Jamie leaned over her shoulder, closer than necessary but she let it slide.

Dear Tony,

My parents are being real knobs. They simply don't understand my friendship with two teen boys and why it's so important. I started at my new school but I haven't connected with anyone and I sit by myself at lunch. I really miss you and Lary...

Davis paused. "What was your grandfather's first name again?"

"Lawrence."

"Could that be Lary?"

"Possibly." He frowned. "My family never could spell."

She kept reading. The letter rambled adorably about school lunch, annoying teachers, and the book she was currently obsessed with. Then—

She froze. "With love, Davis."

Jamie's eyebrows shot up. "Wait. She had your name?"

"I have her name," Davis whispered, stunned. "Was I named after her?"

"Did your mom ever mention it?"

"No. I asked once. She said she couldn't remember but liked the sound of it."

"I was named after a book character," he said. "My mother brought it up at every holiday. And dentist appointment. And once at a gas station. Strange yours didn't remember."

"Yes, strange," she murmured. "Okay. Letter two."

This one came with pictures. A teenage girl smiling shyly at the camera. The same girl from the attic photo.

Jamie squinted. "You two look similar. Same nose. Same 'I hate mornings' eyes."

"My grandmother never liked me," Davis said. "But she never liked my father either and I look like him. I don't see how I could be related to this Davis."

"Resembling someone doesn't automatically make you related," he said, trying to be reassuring but failing due to the fact he was already comparing their ears.

"Maybe what she wrote will clarify things."

Davis began reading again.

Dear Tony,

I hate my sister. Evelyn has done her best to stop me from even being able to write you. Please don't ever fall in love with her. She would make you a horrible wife...

When she finished, Jamie let out a theatrical gasp. "Who is Evelyn?"

"My great-grand aunt, I think? Though everyone called her Eve."

"The plot thickens," he declared dramatically, waving his coffee like a wand.

"Careful," she warned. "You're sloshing."

He licked the coffee from his fingers. Davis's insides clenched when she thought about what Jamie liked to do with his tongue when they were in bed.

Stop, she told herself. She pulled out the third envelope. This one had nothing groundbreaking, so she grabbed the fourth. Then the fifth.

After the tenth, she dropped backward onto the carpet with a groan. "My brain is melting."

Jamie stretched with a grunt. "My brain melted after the second one. The third letter was just emotional overtime."

She smacked his arm. "You're impossible."

"I know," he said proudly, then nudged her knee with his. "Break?"

"Break."

They sat there in comfortable silence, surrounded by letters, tea, coffee, family secrets, and a growing sense that the past had somehow woven their paths together long before they ever met, though she kept that particular observation very, very quiet. For now.

Chapter Thirty-Six

JAMIE

Dinner had been an adventure. Which was a polite way of describing Davis lecturing him on how quinoa was "a protein powerhouse" while he quietly wondered whether the ancient Incas truly meant for it to taste like damp gravel. But he ate it. Every last miniscule grain.

Then there was the tempeh she prepared. He took a bite after examining it carefully. At least it wasn't tofu.

"I hate to ask what this is besides delicious, but I'm asking?"

Davis smiled. "It's tofu that has fermented into mold. It's very high in protein."

Why did he ask? He knew better. He was eating mold and complementing the chef on how good the mold tasted.

Aliens had to have taken over his body and replaced him with an anti-meat alien.

Now, with the dishes drying and the house quiet except for the sleepy hum of the old estate settling for the night, they returned to the dining room where the letters waited.

Davis curled into her reading spot but this time added a pillow and blanket along with her tea, and Jamie sat beside her in what had become his reading spot: slightly too close, like he needed to make sure she didn't drown in excessive literary exposure.

She held up the next envelope. "Ready for round two?"

"Define 'ready,'" he said. "If it involves emotional turmoil, no. If it involves finding out your ancestor had a secret alien family or a pirate phase, count me in."

She gave him a flat look. "Letters."

"Right. Emotional turmoil it is."

She opened the next envelope and removed two photos. One of Tony, one of Lary. Both young, both grinning, both looking like the kind of guys who could talk a police officer out of a ticket simply by existing.

"I can't believe they were friends before your grandfather became my uncle's butler," Davis murmured.

"Maybe this letter clears things up," Jamie offered. "Or makes it worse. Fifty-fifty shot."

She smirked at him and began reading.

It was more of the same so she quickly went to the next letter and then the next. Finally, she came to Davis's senior year in high school.

Dear Tony,

Lary says you're being dramatic again. I told him that's a requirement for you. Honestly, I miss you both so much my chest hurts. College cannot come soon enough. It's so close I can smell it.

I promise I'll write more soon. I've been so busy with the school newspaper and I finally found my people. Don't worry, none of them replace you or Lary. But there's something I need to tell you. Something big. Something I hope won't make you hate me.

With all my love, Davis

Davis lowered the letter slowly.

"Oh damn," Jamie breathed. "This is the 'big reveal' chapter, isn't it? The one all the TV shows put right before the midseason finale."

"Shh." She unfolded another envelope.

This one was thicker, stuffed with a longer letter and a folded Polaroid. She lifted the picture first.

It was an old snapshot of the girl, Davis's namesake, sitting on a picnic blanket between Tony and Lary. The men gazed at her like she was the sun. Or dessert.

Jamie let out a low whistle. "They were both in love with her."

"Obviously," she murmured.

The envelope trembled ever so slightly before she read.

Dear Tony,

I should've told you sooner but I was afraid. You and Lary, you both love me. Anyone could see it. And you're both wonderful. Truly. The best friends a girl could have.

But I can't be what you want.

I don't love boys. Not like that.

I think I'm in love with Stacy who works on the school newspaper with me. Please don't be mad. Please don't stop writing. I don't want to lose you. Either of you. Stacy wants to go to college with us. You will love her after you get over hating her.

With honesty, and still with love,

Davis

Davis stopped. Her breath snagged. She pressed her palm to her chest.

Jamie sat forward, elbows on his knees. "She was gay."

"Yes," Davis whispered. "Yes she was."

"That's why she avoided marrying either of them," he said gently. "Why she didn't want her parents deciding her life. Why she wanted college so badly."

Davis folded the letter once, twice, placed it carefully on the table, and picked up the next one. The reply.

Her hands trembled for real now, so Jamie reached out and covered her fingers with his.

"You okay?" he murmured.

She nodded, but her eyes were glassy. "Just feels like I've found someone I didn't know existed but somehow always knew."

"Then," he said softly, "let's meet the rest of her."

She took a shaky breath, opened the next envelope, and began.

Dear Davis,

I'm not mad. You should've told me sooner, yes, but mad? Never. You're our Davis. Mine and Lary's. No matter what. If anything, I'm mad we let you carry this alone.

We love you, not just the version we wanted you to be. The real you.

And your friend? If she doesn't treat you right, Lary says he'll challenge her to some kind of honor duel. I told him that's dumb. He told me I'm dumb. So nothing is new.

Please write soon.

Tony

An unexpected laugh burst out of Davis. "An honor duel," she snorted. "Of course."

Jamie grinned. "My ancestors were dramatic as hell."

"And loyal," she added softly. "So loyal."

The next envelope held a letter addressed to both men at once.

Then another. And another. They didn't go to college together and Stacy became a thing of the past very soon. But Davis did go to college and she told them stories of no longer wanting to hide the fact she liked girls. She wrote of heartbreak when her next lover left and of discovering herself in ways she never could under her parents' roof.

They read until Davis's voice turned hoarse and Jamie's coffee went cold.

When she could read no longer, she leaned back on her elbows, mentally exhausted.

Jamie studied her profile. "You okay?"

"Yes," she whispered. "Better than okay. It's like I'm named after someone who fought to be who she really was. Someone brave. Someone who didn't let anyone crush her."

Jamie rubbed the back of his neck, suddenly shy. "Fits you. Are you gay?"

It was asked casually.

"Let me think about it." One second, two, three. "Nope, I like men."

"That's a relief."

She gave him a long lingering glance.

A moment passed until Jamie cleared his throat and ruined it, because he was him.

"So," he said, "are you ready for the next batch tomorrow?"

She smiled, tired but glowing. "Yes. I want to know what happened to her. To all of them."

She looked directly into his eyes. "Can I sleep in your bed tonight?"

His hand came out and he ran his fingers across her cheek. "I was hoping you would."

Chapter Thirty-Seven

DAVIS

Morning sunlight filtered through the greenhouse windows. They had decided to read the last letters there. It seemed appropriate.

The box sat between them again. Davis had brewed tea for herself, coffee for Jamie, and it was time to read.

Davis, Lary, and Tony had all graduated college and moved on in their lives. Their friendship remained strong. The men remained in love with Davis but respected her. The letters told about their lives and even mentioned Tony's growing infatuation with Evelyn.

"This is it," Davis whispered. "The last four letters. Now it seems like there should be so many more and that scares me."

Jamie nodded like he understood and took a slow breath. "You sure you're ready?"

"Nope," she said honestly. "But when has that ever stopped me?"

"Fair point." He nudged her leg with his. "Let's rip off the emotional Band-Aid."

She picked up the first of the final four. The paper felt older, like it had been handled many times.

Dear Tony,

I didn't want to tell you this. I didn't want to tell Lary either, but he forced it out of me and now you need to know.

I'm sick.

It started with fatigue and bruises, but now it's more. The doctors say it's aggressive. They're trying everything, but they won't promise anything except "more tests."

I'm scared. But I'm trying not to be. I don't want to waste what time I have wishing for more of it.

Davis put the letter down slowly.

Jamie didn't speak. He just reached for her knee and rested his hand there.

She swallowed hard and grabbed the next envelope.

Dear Tony,

Please tell Lary I'm okay. He keeps calling and asking if I need a kidney or something. I told him kidneys don't fix this. He told me he has two and I can take one anyway.

You boys. Always trying to fix things with body parts and questionable logic.

My roommate moved out. I don't blame her. I've been in and out of the hospital. I think seeing me like this scares people. I'm trying not to let it scare me too.

I miss you both.

You were always the brave ones. I'm trying to be brave too.

Jamie exhaled shakily. "She still had humor."

"She was probably trying to keep them from falling apart," Davis whispered.

Jamie looked at her questioningly, but she pretended not to notice.

She opened the third envelope.

Dear Tony,

They know now. My parents. I had to tell them. I hate how sad they looked. I hate how helpless everyone feels. Even with my life choices that they don't agree with, they love me. I was worried they no longer did but I've been proved wrong. I'm moving back in with them because I can't do this alone anymore.

I didn't think about it before but I won't ever find my other half. I won't have the life I thought I was growing toward.

But I'm not sorry. Not for who I am. Not for loving who I loved.

Please don't be sad for me. Please don't stop living because I'm dying.

I want you and Lary to be happy. Truly. You've given me more joy than you'll ever understand.

Davis set this letter down more carefully than the others. Her throat felt tight. Her heart ached in a way she couldn't fully explain, as if she were mourning someone she'd known and loved forever.

Jamie was silent, but his hand found hers. He didn't squeeze. He didn't tug. He just held.

Only the last envelope remained.

The flap was uneven, the ink slightly faded. Davis's fingers trembled as she opened it.

Dear Tony,

This will be short. I'm tired today.

I had a dream that the three of us were old. Gray and wrinkled and arguing about something ridiculous, like whether soup counts as a beverage. Lary insisted it did. You kept telling him it was a "wet food" and he said that made it sound like cat chow.

I woke up laughing. I miss laughing with you both.

If this is my last letter, please know: you mattered. You mattered so much. More than you ever knew.

I'm not afraid now. Not anymore. I've loved deeply. I've lived honestly. I hope you do the same.

Davis

A heavy silence followed.

"There's another note tucked into the envelope," Davis said, wiping her cheek. She opened it.

Davis and Jamie,

Davis died a few days after her last letter. You have no idea how much we loved her. Because of her sexual persuasion, she never had to choose between me and Lawrence. It allowed us to remain lifelong friends. He was so much more than a butler and honestly I was jealous that he died first and got to be with Davis again before me. But I'm with her now. I loved my wife but sadly, I loved Davis more.

I set up this entire mad scheme to reel you both in. You are a reflection of me and Davis and Lawrence. Both your mothers kept Lawrence and I appraised of your lives. Honestly, the entire idea was Lary's though I wished I had thought of it first.

You're getting closer to one year. We have something special planned for the holidays.

Uncle Tony

"This is heartbreaking," Davis said. "She never got to finish her life. I hate that."

Jamie slid closer until their shoulders touched. "But she lived it right. That's something."

"She died alone."

"No." His voice was gentle. "She died loved."

Davis looked at the fan of envelopes, feeling a strange mixture of grief and gratitude.

"I can't believe my mother never told me," she whispered.

"Maybe she didn't know the details." Jamie brushed a stray tear from her cheek with the softest touch she'd ever felt from him.

She didn't pull away.

For a long moment, they sat in silence, surrounded by the final words of a girl who had lived bravely, loved fiercely, and left behind echoes that felt eerily, beautifully familiar.

Finally, Jamie nudged her shoulder.

"So," he said softly, "what do you want to do now?"

Davis sniffed and leaned into him. "It's like the story is still unfinished."

Jamie looked out the greenhouse window seemingly in deep thought but he didn't say anything.

Chapter Thirty-Eight

DAVIS

For several days, things around the house felt muted. The light bantering between her and Jamie was missing.

And sadly, Davis knew it was her fault.

She was madly in love with him.

He was infatuated and turned on by her. Oh, she was turned on to the point of constant combustion, but for her, it was so much more than that. The circumstances they were in were grossly unfair. Her great-uncle had no idea what would happen between them. Or maybe he did and he thought it would be fun to stir up their love life.

She decided she needed to set things straight. She had to stop her love feelings where they stood. Being pressed up against six feet of mountain man who kissed like he was sculpted by Greek gods for sinful purposes was not helping her heart.

She pushed off the couch after they watched a movie together and wrapped her arms around herself. "I need boundaries."

Jamie, still sitting with one arm propped over the back of the couch like he owned gravity, blinked. "Huh?"

"Boundaries," she repeated. "Like, actual ones. Fences. Imaginary lines in metaphorical sand. Pick whichever metaphor makes you least confused."

"I'm still confused," he admitted. "Why do we need boundaries now? We just watched a movie together. That feels like the opposite of boundaries."

She paced the room. "That's the problem."

"Movies are the problem?"

"No, Jamie." She stopped, whirled around, and pointed at him. "You."

He straightened a little, clearly alarmed. "Me?"

"Yes. You!" Her voice cracked. "I'm falling for you more and more each day. That was not in the binding contractual agreement for one year of cohabitation and joint estate management."

Jamie blinked like a man trying to solve a puzzle with only corner pieces. "Wait. Falling for me is bad?"

She threw her hands up. "It's terrible!"

He stared. "I'm sorry, what?"

"Because," she pressed on, pacing again, "you treat me like I'm your comfort dessert!"

His brows furrowed. "Dessert is good. I don't see the problem."

"I am not pudding, Jamie!"

He held up his hands. "I have never once implied you were pudding. Besides, pudding isn't vegan and I would not compare you to carnivore food."

"You know what I mean." Her voice softened, trying to get her point across to him. "After this year is up, we go our separate ways. You to your hunting cabin or whatever manly retreat you crawl into, and me to whatever my life is supposed to be. We can assign months for house visits so our paths don't cross. I don't want to be your casual hookup. Your—your fuck-buddy."

Jamie inhaled sharply, shoulders stiffening. "I've never called you that."

"You don't have to." She wrapped her arms around herself again, suddenly cold. "I can feel it. And I can't do that. I can't do this," she twirled her finger in the air, "if I'm going to walk away in a few months with my heart shredded."

Jamie stood so fast the blanket fell off the couch.

"Stop," he said roughly.

"No. I need to say this."

"You don't know what I think," he said, stepping closer.

"And you don't say what you feel!" she snapped. "Which is the entire problem!"

He took another step forward. "Davis."

"No," she said again. "I need a boundary. A big one. I need to know that after this year, we're done. Clean break. No lingering sex. No backslide. No late-night 'hey I'm in town' texts."

Jamie flinched like she'd slapped him. "Why would you think I'd treat you like that?"

"Because you've never said otherwise!"

He stared at her as though his brain had short-circuited. Then, with the stunned disbelief of a man discovering the world was round, he said, "Davis, I am not using you."

"I didn't say you were."

"Yes, you did," he said, his voice rising. "You said you thought I wanted you to be some convenient arrangement! A drive-thru girlfriend I could visit when I felt lonely!"

"Well, what am I supposed to think?" she shot back. "You keep everything locked up like Fort Knox! You never talk about what's happening between us! You never say what you want beyond tonight!"

"Because I didn't know if you wanted me for more than short term!"

They froze.

The words hung between them.

Davis's breath caught. "Of course I want you. That's the whole damn problem."

Jamie let out a ragged laugh that wasn't really a laugh. "I thought you were holding back. Keeping things casual because it was easier. I thought if I said too much, I'd scare you off."

"You don't scare me," she whispered.

"Then why the hell would you think I'd toss you away at the end of the year?"

"Because everyone else has."

Jamie took one more step, so close her breath came faster. "I'm not everyone else," he said softly. "I need you to understand that."

Tears welled in her stupid, traitorous eyes. "I just don't want to end this year broken by love that isn't returned."

"I don't want this year to end, period," he returned, voice barely a whisper.

Her heart stumbled.

He reached for her hand; slow enough she could pull away. She didn't.

"Davis," he murmured, "if you need boundaries, we'll have boundaries. If you need clarity, I'll give you clarity. But don't," his voice cracked, "don't push me out because you think I'm not all in."

She blinked up at him. "Are you?"

"In so deeply I can't climb out," he said simply.

Something in her chest detonated into warmth and she stepped into him, because her heart had already leapt.

And Jamie exhaled, forehead falling against hers as if gravity demanded they meet.

No kiss.

No heat.

Just closeness. Bare, emotional, real.

A moment that promised there would be choices to make. Hard ones.

But for now, they simply breathed together.

Chapter Thirty-Nine

JAMIE

He was convinced of one thing: Women did not come with instruction manuals.

If they did, Jamie's copy was missing at least twelve chapters and a few supplemental diagrams. He wasn't alone in this. Hell, he was pretty sure most men were wandering around confused, pretending they weren't confused, and hoping no one asked follow-up questions.

Take Davis, for example.

He ate her vegan food without complaint. He watched documentaries about fish having feelings (or whatever point the documentary had been trying to make). He even delayed plans for his next hunt because it would make her sad.

Sad.

He couldn't stand the look she got, those big eyes going soft and wounded like a Disney deer watching a forest fire. It annihilated him.

And it wasn't even a normal hunt he was delaying. This was the good one, the ecological one, a controlled deer-tag season with other hunters who donated the meat, helped with herd balance, and felt all noble about doing something that was technically murder but ethically beneficial.

The kind of hunt he loved.

And still, Jamie felt guilty.

Guilty.

About taking a hike with weapons in the woods.

He scrubbed his hands over his face and glared out the window like the trees owed him an explanation.

According to the will, he had a seventy-two-hour alone limit. He could only leave the estate without Davis for three days, and that wasn't enough time to scout the land, line up good positions or finish the hunt.

Another reason to feel guilty.

Damn.

He didn't want to see the sadness in her eyes. He didn't want her thinking he cared more about a hunt than about her. He didn't know when that shift had happened and his priority list quietly rearranged itself and put Davis at the top like she'd always belonged there, but it had.

He also thought they had an understanding. Something real. Something more than "friends who occasionally tumble into bed like horny mice in a cheese factory."

But Davis had rules. Boundaries. Complicated emotional systems Jamie struggled to connect the dots on. He hated feelings, absolutely despised them, but around her, feelings spilled out of him like a ruptured sieve.

His man card had officially been replaced with tofu.

And there was no getting around it.

He was staring at the hunt map on his screen, trying to figure out how screwed his timeline was, when Davis swept into the room like a tiny vegan hurricane.

"Did you know that human carnivore poop stinks and vegan poop has an almost sweet smell?" she announced.

No greeting. No preamble. Just that.

Clovis toddled to her on her absurd little chicken feet, making soft clucks of affection as Davis scooped her up.

Jamie closed his laptop with the resigned dread of a man who knew he wasn't getting out of this conversation alive.

"We talk about it," Davis continued, stroking Clovis. "Us vegans. It's a thing. And let me tell you, meat eaters can smell up a bathroom faster than a constipated skunk discovering coffee."

Jamie pinched the bridge of his nose. "Are we really doing this? Are we having a bowel-movement discussion? Because that's something old people do, and I am not old."

She gave him a look. One of those *bless your heart, you sweet dumb creature* looks. "I was dusting the front room and poop crossed my mind. I thought you should know."

"You're telling me vegan shit doesn't stink?"

"Not in the same way carnivore shit does." She said it completely seriously, like she'd performed peer-reviewed research on the matter.

He changed the subject because talking about fecal bouquets wasn't helping his already fragile mental state. "I read somewhere before meeting you that vegans think they're better than everyone else," he said. It didn't go as he expected.

"We are."

Zero shame.

Zero hesitation.

Like she was stating that water was wet and the sky was blue.

"Why?"

"We don't torture some animal in order to eat," she said simply. "Of course we're better."

Jamie rubbed his beard, which was usually how he signaled his brain needed a jump-start. "You know that's why people hate you, right?"

"So?" She shrugged, still petting Clovis. "I don't care what meat eaters say about me. Most of it isn't true anyway."

"You just said your superiority was true."

"Yes," she agreed. "Because it is. But the rest? Like that protein and iron nonsense you went on and on about when we first moved in together. Please. You've put on muscle since being here, so clearly you aren't wasting away. And I haven't heard you screaming for fresh blood in the middle of the night, so your iron must be fine. Those are falsehoods spread by the meat and dairy industry."

She buried her hand into Clovis's side feathers. "And look at you, because you connected with one chicken, you took chickens off your eat list. That's compassion, Jamie. Why can't you connect the dots to all the other animals raised for slaughter and what it entails?"

He shrugged. "Because I'm a meat eater."

"And that's why I'm better than you."

She set Clovis down with all the grace of a queen setting down a royal child.

Then she huffed.

Then she spun around.

Then she marched dramatically out of the room and slammed the door behind her.

Jamie stared at the closed door, stunned.

He replayed the conversation.

The poop talk.

The superiority declaration.

The dramatic exit.

He slowly blinked.

"Was that our first fight?"

Clovis clucked once.

Jamie took that as a yes.

Chapter Forty

JAMIE

He used to love this. The crisp morning air. The quiet. The smell of pine mixed with cold earth. The anticipation of the hunt. He understood herd management. Real conservation work.

He used to feel comfortable out here.

Now he felt nauseous.

Partly because Davis insisted on eating some kind of spirulina breakfast paste in the truck and it smelled like fermented sea moss, and partly because she was sitting beside him humming cheerfully, for God's sake, on the way to a deer hunt.

She didn't belong here.

He shouldn't have brought her but the will took that issue out of his hands. And she insisted. Said something about "observing the enemy in their natural habitat," which he thought was a joke but was beginning to realize was actually a battle plan.

And now, walking up the trail with his rifle slung over his shoulder and four seasoned hunters behind him, Jamie could feel his stomach coil into knots. Because Davis was behind him, narrating her thoughts out loud like she was filming a nature documentary no one asked for.

"And that is a deer track," she whispered loudly enough for birds two counties over to hear. "Which means they're close. Which means you monsters are going to try to shoot Bambi's cousin."

One of the hunters, Rick, tall, bearded, built like a northern lumberjack, glanced at Jamie. "You brought her?" he mouthed.

Jamie gave an apologetic shrug. "She insisted," he mouthed back.

Rick shook his head in sympathy. "Condolences," he whispered.

They reached a ridge where the group paused to view the valley. The morning sun spilled over the hills, lighting the brush in amber. It was beautiful. Jamie used to feel a surge of purpose at this sight.

Now?

He mostly felt like vomiting.

Because every time he looked at a deer, he saw, well, a deer.

With a face.

And feelings.

And probably a favorite tree or something.

He blamed Davis entirely.

"Gentlemen!" Davis called out suddenly, planting herself in front of the group like a motivational speaker preparing to ruin the economy of beef jerky sales nationwide.

All four hunters froze.

"Before you slaughter anything today," she said with dramatic flair, "I would like to discuss the moral, ethical, and emotional implications of your actions."

The hunters just stared.

There went his tip. Again.

Eyes drifted between Davis, her rainbow knit beanie, and Clovis tucked into her backpack like a baby in a papoose.

One of the men, Tim, blinked. "Is that a chicken?"

"Yes," Davis said proudly. "She's here to witness."

"Oh," Tim said faintly. "I thought she might be dinner."

Jamie wished the ground would swallow him.

After giving Tim a killing glare, Davis launched into her speech.

"Deer have families! They have community. They mourn. They feel pain. They feel connection. They have best friends. Do you have best friends? I bet you do. And does someone hunt them?"

Rick leaned toward Jamie and whispered, "Should we answer?"

"No," Jamie muttered. "Do not engage."

But it was too late, Davis was winding up like a vegan tsunami.

"Consider their emotional well-being. Imagine if someone shot you while you were peacefully grazing on wildflowers."

Rick frowned. "I don't graze."

"You eat!" Davis snapped. "Same thing!"

Jamie rubbed his forehead. The headache forming behind his eyes felt like a small, angry woodpecker.

The hunters exchanged uncomfortable glances.

Finally, Hank, the oldest, slowest, calmest of the bunch, cleared his throat.

"Ma'am, with all due respect," he drawled kindly, "the deer around here are overpopulated. They're starving, they carry disease, and they're damaging the ecosystem. We're helping."

"You're helping yourselves so you can wear your macho pants in public!" Davis countered. "For shooting them!"

Hank shrugged. "Also true."

Jamie pinched the bridge of his nose again. He was getting permanent lines caused by this woman.

Davis stepped forward, hands on hips. "Tell me," she said. "How can you justify killing something so innocent?"

Rick opened his mouth, paused, and then held up a finger. "Actually, Jamie? You're the talker. You answer."

Jamie startled. "Why me?"

"Because we're paying you to find us those deer and to answer the questions from the," he waved at Davis, "whatever she is, and you brought her on our hunt."

"Whatever she is?" Jamie sputtered. "She's simply a vegan."

The men's faces twisted into looks of horror at the word.

Davis crossed her arms. "Answer the question, Jamie."

Oh hell.

Jamie cleared his throat. "Well, uh, it's for conservation. And deer population control. And, uh."

A young buck appeared at the tree line.

Davis gasped. The hunters perked up. Jamie froze.

The deer lifted its head, ears twitching, big eyes shining, looking so damn innocent, it could've been the poster child for *Please Don't Kill Me Magazine*.

Normally, Jamie would have someone take a shot.

Today?

He couldn't do it.

Rick stared at him. "Seriously?"

Jamie swallowed hard. "I'm thinking."

"You don't think," Rick said flatly. "You point and we shoot."

Davis looked at Jamie like he had sprouted angel wings.

His stomach twisted. He'd never felt so torn in his life.

Rick raised his rifle.

Davis shrieked like someone had electrocuted her.

"No!" she lunged at Rick's arm like a rabid ferret.

Rick yelped, jolted, and the bullet shot harmlessly into the dirt three feet from his own boot.

"Woman!" he barked. "You can't do that!"

"You were about to commit murder!"

"It's not murder!" Rick protested. "It's a deer!"

The entire valley went silent.

Even the wind paused.

Clovis let out a confused little cluck.

Rick shot Jamie a look. "Control your vegan."

"She's not my—"

But the words stuck, because she was kind of his.

Davis glared at all of them, hands on hips, righteous glare on full display. "You're all wrong," she declared. "You don't know them like I do."

"They're deer," Hank said, as if breaking bad news.

"They have names!" Davis insisted.

"No they don't," Jamie started.

"Yes they do," she said, turning toward the buck. She pointed dramatically. "That one is Frank."

The buck blinked.

"His name is not Frank," Rick said, bewildered.

"Frank deserves to live!" Davis proclaimed.

Rick, Tim, Hank, and Pete all stared at Frank.

Then at Davis.

Then at Jamie.

Finally, Hank sighed. "Son, I think your lady is having a moment."

"I think she is," Jamie said weakly.

Davis didn't even glance his way. She was still glaring at the forest like she could vegan-chant the bullets into soybeans.

And here was the damning part: Jamie didn't want Frank to die either.

Not today.

Not with her here.

Not with the weird ache in his chest.

Hank lowered his rifle. "Alright, we're taking lunch early. We'll reconvene after her episode ends."

Davis huffed, triumphant. "Episode? I call it enlightenment."

The hunters trudged away.

Jamie stood beside her, staring at the trees where Frank had vanished.

"You know," he said quietly, "that was dangerous."

She crossed her arms. "So is shooting Frank."

He exhaled. "His name is not Frank."

"It is to me."

And dammit. Jamie smiled. He didn't mean to. But he did.

Because she was ridiculous.

And impossible.

And wonderful.

And he was absolutely ruined.

He knew, with unsettling clarity, that today was the first day he hadn't enjoyed a hunt. Not even a little.

Because every deer now had a name.

And feelings.

And possibly a favorite tree.

And it was all Davis's fault.

She looked up at him, hazel eyes fierce under that rainbow beanie. "You're thinking differently," she said quietly.

"Yeah," he admitted.

"You're seeing them."

He let out a long breath. "Yeah."

She smiled with no smugness.

And Jamie realized something terrifying: He needed a new career.

Chapter Forty-One

DAVIS

She had always believed her words carried weight. Maybe not enough to change the world, but enough to make someone pause. Enough to make someone see.

But out there on that hunt, Davis's words hadn't carried anything.

The hunters still shot three deer.

Including Frank.

She cried for them that night inside the tent, curled on her sleeping bag with her back to everyone and her heart feeling like someone had stepped on it repeatedly. She refused to sit with the men, refused their food, refused their attempts at small talk. The cheerful roar of their post-hunting celebration felt like nails scraping her insides.

Clovis scratched around the tent floor for a while, pecking at imaginary crumbs before giving up and hopping into Davis's arms. The hen tucked herself under Davis's chin, a quiet presence in the dark.

"I think Jamie needs a pig," Davis whispered to her through tears. "A smart one. Big brown eyes. Knows how to sit. If he could see how terrified pigs are before slaughter, how aware, they wouldn't just be bacon to him. He'd see them the way he sees you."

Clovis blinked sleepily. Chickens didn't do sympathy. But she stayed, which was enough.

When a drunk Jamie finally stumbled into the tent an hour later, the smell of whiskey and woodsmoke clinging to him, Davis rolled away and pretended to be asleep. They didn't speak. They didn't touch. The space between them felt wider than the entire forest.

They left before sunrise.

Five hours in the truck, and she could count their words on one hand. Davis was tired, heartsick, and emotionally hollow. When they got back to the house, she heated a vegan processed dinner that tasted like cardboard sadness, and Jamie ate it without a single complaint.

She didn't even have the energy to tease him for it.

The next day, she retreated to the greenhouse and stayed there for hours, kneeling in the dirt, trying to realign her heart. Clovis pecked happily for grubs but Davis was too sad to hum, too wounded to enjoy singing.

The image of those three deer haunted her every time she closed her eyes.

Could she really build a life with someone who took another life so casually?

She hated the word *carnivore*. Humans weren't carnivores. They were omnivores. And if she heard one more person claim they needed meat for iron or protein, she might scream. Almost everything needed for survival came from the soil; vegans simply cut out the middleman and the torture. That was all.

But how could Jamie connect with a chicken and go blind to all the other species?

Footsteps crunched outside.

Speak of the devil.

Jamie stepped into the greenhouse; hands shoved deep in his pockets. "Another box came for us."

Her pulse jumped. "Where is it?"

"Dining room."

"Let me wash my hands first."

He nodded, but lingered there awkwardly, glancing around the greenhouse like he wasn't sure if he was welcome inside it anymore.

"I can't believe how well this place is doing," he said finally. "Are all these plants edible?"

Did he actually care, or was he trying to earn Good Boy Points?

"They're edible," she answered cautiously.

He walked to the basil, brushed his fingers over the leaves. "You've done an amazing job in here. Your uncle would be proud of you."

She brightened a little despite herself. That felt real.

"Thank you."

Silence stretched between them.

Finally, she exhaled. "I'm sorry I ruined you getting a tip from those hunters."

"It's fine," he said. "They still gave me a good one."

She blinked. "They did?"

"Yeah." He hesitated. "And I'm sorry you were put in a position that goes against everything you believe in. It's unfair."

Her chest softened. "Thank you. I guess this sucks for both of us."

She almost added, *it sucked more for the deer*, but she swallowed the words.

Jamie seemed to realize that. He swallowed too.

"Let's see what's in the box," he said gently.

They walked to the dining room together, a little closer than before, but not fully back in step. Davis approached the large cardboard box on the table.

Their names were typed neatly on a label on the front.

Her heart fluttered.

"Ready?" Jamie asked.

"No," she admitted. "But let's pretend I am."

He sliced the tape with his pocketknife and stepped back so she could lift the flaps.

Inside, tissue paper shimmered in a deep rich red.

She reached in and pulled out a dress. A stunning floor-length gown made of satin and magic. A deep red ballgown with a fitted bodice and a swooping neckline. The fabric caught the light, glowing like a glass of wine.

"Oh," Davis breathed. "This is gorgeous."

Jamie lifted the next item, a sleek black tuxedo, perfectly pressed, tailored, and wrapped in a garment bag.

"Well damn," he murmured. "Is this for me?"

"It better be," she said. "I'm not wearing it."

He chuckled softly, her first time hearing him laugh since before the hunt, and it warmed her unexpectedly.

Beneath the clothes were two envelopes.

Jamie handed over the first one.

Inside were two glossy tickets to the Cherrywood Charity Winter Ball. Elegant script, silver embossing, the works.

She blinked. "This takes place the week before Christmas."

"The fancy kind of ball," Jamie said, staring at the tux like it might bite. "Where I'm pretty sure you're not allowed to bring a chicken."

Davis ignored him and opened the second envelope, the one from the attorney. A single letter lay inside, handwritten in her uncle Anthony's looping script.

My Dearest Davis,

If you are reading this, then you have reached the point in your inheritance where you can begin stepping back into the world.

Enclosed are two things: the dress is a perfect replica of one my Davis wore to her senior prom. Lary and I escorted her together.

Go to the Winter Ball. Have fun. Dance. Laugh. Live. This estate wasn't meant to isolate you; it was meant to help you find your way back to yourself.

And make Jamie dance with you. No one should dance alone.

With love,

Uncle Anthony

P.S. This was only a note.

Davis stared at the note.

Jamie watched her, something unreadable in his eyes. "So," he said lightly, "I guess we're going to a ball."

She looked up, heart twisting, still hurting after the hunt. But also, hopeful.

"We are," she said.

Even though a part of her wondered if dancing with him would make being in love with him harder.

Chapter Forty-Two

DAVIS

Davis was ninety percent sure her spine had fused into a permanent stoop from hauling produce. Tomatoes, squash, peppers, onions, herbs—her entire life had turned into a never-ending parade of vegetables marching toward canning jars and freezer bags like soldiers on deployment.

And she still had three planters to go.

The greenhouse felt like it was breathing. Humid air puffed warm against her skin, fogging the glass panes while late-afternoon sun streaked through the hanging vines. Uncle Anthony's sanctuary had exploded into a lush, wild, overachieving Eden, and Davis loved it. She loved the earth smell, the tangled clusters of cherry tomatoes, the way basil brushed her fingers when she passed.

What she did not love was the six-foot menace standing at the canning station that included a small woodburning stove, a sink, and a blender. Jamie frowned at the jar in his hands, then at her, then at it again. "I'm just saying," he said stubbornly, "this feels unhealthy." He held the mason jar like it was a live grenade.

"It's real food." Davis wiped sweat from her forehead with the back of her wrist. "The way they prepared food in the good old days, and it's food you're going to eat."

"After you boil it," he said, "seal it, and maybe hex it."

She paused. "Hex it?"

"Look at this thing!" He lifted the jar as if offering it to the gods. Inside sat diced tomatoes, neatly packed and bubbling from heat. "It's steaming. Inside glass. Glass shouldn't steam. I'm pretty sure glass shouldn't do half the things you're making it do."

"It's science."

"It's witchcraft."

"You grew up hunting, Jamie. You're telling me that canning vegetables is where you draw the line?"

"Yes," he said solemnly. "Because vegetables shouldn't try to kill you after they've been cooked."

"They're not going to kill you."

He pointed at the jars cooling on the counter by the large outdoor stove. "They're clicking. I can smell botulism."

"They're sealing and you do not smell botulism."

"I do too!"

Davis laughed. It was an undignified snort she couldn't hold back. "You're ridiculous."

"I'm cautious." He crossed his arms. "They hissed at me."

"They did not hiss at you."

"Maybe it was more of a pop." He grimaced. "A threatening pop."

She reached for a ripe tomato still clinging to the vine and plucked it free. "Okay, tough guy, since you're so brave in the forest, let's see you tackle the dangerous task of washing and dicing more tomatoes."

He didn't move. He squinted at the tomato in her hand like it was armed.

"Davis," he said. "I don't trust produce that can explode under pressure."

"It wasn't exploding. It was venting air."

"You know what explodes under pressure?" he interrupted. "Guns."

"Not the same."

"Feels like the same."

She shoved the tomato into his palm. "Wash. Cut."

He took it like a man accepting his fate.

They worked side by side for a while. Jamie muttered under his breath about the inherent danger of "vegetable bombs," Davis quietly enjoying the way sunlight kept finding him. He'd rolled his sleeves up, revealing tan forearms she'd absolutely-not-on-purpose noticed too many times today. And yesterday. And maybe the day before.

He cut tomatoes like they were unstable uranium. She didn't tease him. Much.

When they had enough to fill another six jars, she slid the tomatoes into a bowl.

"You don't have to help," she said softly.

"Yes, I do," he said, equally soft. Then, because he had to ruin it: "Apparently if you don't harvest all this in time, it turns into compost, and then I have to spread the compost. So really? This is self-preservation."

She nudged him with her hip. "Every day with you is a gift."

"You're welcome."

The sun dipped lower, turning the greenhouse another shade of gold. Dust and pollen sparkled in the beams. Outside, the crisp hint of autumn wind rattled branches and carried the scent of the forest.

Her uncle had made all this. And it was close to being hers. The thought still sat strangely on her shoulders.

Jamie watched her too closely sometimes, like he could see the thoughts she didn't say.

"You okay?" he asked.

She nodded, but she didn't look at him. "Just thinking."

"Dangerous," he said lightly.

She rolled her eyes. "You're hilarious."

"Tell me what's going on up there." He tapped her temple with a tomato juice-free finger.

She hesitated, then exhaled. "I'm trying really hard not to mess this up," she said. "This place, it mattered to him. It's starting to matter to me. And I don't want to ruin anything."

Jamie's expression softened in a way that made her pulse do a thing she definitely didn't authorize.

"You couldn't ruin this if you tried," he said. "You care too much."

She swallowed. "You don't know that."

"Oh, I do." He lifted a jar, turned it so the light caught the glass, and said gently, "You bring things to life, Davis. Even the things that scare you."

She looked at him then. Really looked.

And he, big, stubborn, irritating Jamie, looked almost shy.

The moment stretched.

Then.

POP.

Jamie yelped, dropped the jar to the counter, and cursed loud enough to scare birds out of the nearby trees.

"It sealed!" Davis gasped between laughter. "It just sealed!"

"It threatened me!" he shot back.

"It did not threaten you!"

He pointed a trembling finger at the innocent jar. "It chose violence."

She was laughing so hard she had to bend over the counter. Tears pricked her eyes. Her stomach hurt. And God, it felt good to laugh like this. With him.

Jamie grumbled but she caught the twitch of a smile he tried to hide.

When she finally straightened, still wiping her eyes, he said, "Fine. I'll keep helping. But if one of these jars explodes, you're burying me with honors."

"Scout's honor," she said solemnly.

"You weren't a Scout."

"Still counts."

He shook his head and reached for another jar. "Let's finish before they unionize."

As the last jars cooled and the greenhouse glowed in twilight, Davis felt something she hadn't allowed herself since the last hunting trip: Hope.

Jamie brushed past her to stack the finished jars, and his arm grazed hers burning through her like wildfire.

He looked at her.

She looked at him.

And outside, the wind whispered across the yard like the world already knew what was about to happen.

The jars clicked softly on the counter, settling into their seals like sleepy little creatures, and Davis pressed a hand over her still-aching ribs.

It was so wonderful to laugh today. Really laugh. The kind that cracked open something inside her and let light spill through.

Jamie leaned against the workbench, arms crossed, pretending he wasn't watching her. But he was. He always was.

Sweat darkened the collar of his shirt, and his rolled sleeves exposed strong forearms dusted with tomato juice and a smear of basil. He looked like trouble disguised as a harvest fantasy.

"You good?" he asked.

No. Absolutely not. Not when he was looking at her like that.

"I'm fine," she lied, wiping her palms on her jeans. "Just tired."

He pushed off the bench and stepped toward her. "Yeah. Long day."

She nodded.

He nodded.

And then neither of them moved. Not away, anyway.

The sunset outside tinted the greenhouse glass amber. It painted his cheekbones gold, cast warm shadows along his jaw, and turned his eyes, usually forest-dark, into something softer.

Her heart thudded. Inconveniently loud.

Jamie cleared his throat. "You, uh, you've got something."

He gestured vaguely at her face.

She froze. "Where?"

"Right here." He brushed his thumb gently across her cheek.

Her breath caught. She wasn't sure if she made a sound, but if she did, she hoped it was internal.

His thumb lingered a second longer than necessary.

Then two seconds longer than necessary.

Then definitely too long to qualify as helpful.

Davis swallowed. "Tomato?"

"Maybe," he said quietly.

His hand slipped away, but the warmth stayed, blooming across her skin.

They stood inches apart now, close enough for her to smell him. Pine and something sweet, probably from the greenhouse itself. Every part of her felt aware of every part of him.

Their sexapades always took place late at night but this was different.

She looked up.

Bad idea.

Because he was already looking at her, eyes a little too serious, a little too intent. His breath brushed her forehead. A single curl of hair had fallen loose from her messy attempt at order, and for one insane second, she thought he would smooth it back.

"You okay?" he asked again, softer this time.

She nodded. This time she meant it less.

His gaze flicked to her mouth, briefly, instinctively, before snapping back to her eyes.

Her pulse did a ridiculous somersault.

"It's getting late," he murmured.

"It is."

"We should head in."

"We should."

They didn't move.

Why were they still so shy with each other, Davis wondered.

Jamie's hand lifted, slowly giving her time to stop him, and brushed the piece of hair behind her ear. His fingertips skimmed the edge of her jaw, and a breath shivered out of her.

"Davis."

The sound of her name from him sent heat spiraling through her.

She didn't step back.

He didn't step forward.

But the space between them shifted all the same, tightening like the world was shrinking.

His thumb traced the faintest line along her jaw. Not a kiss. Not even close. But somehow so much more sensual.

Her voice came out hushed. "Thank you for helping today."

He huffed a small laugh that wasn't a laugh at all. "I'd help you with anything."

Something unspoken hung between them.

Then another jar popped loudly on the counter.

They both jumped.

Jamie swore. Davis clapped a hand over her mouth. And whatever had been about to happen loosened just enough to let them breathe again.

Jamie grabbed her before she grabbed him and they went to the dirt floor, not caring. Clothes came off and laughter continued as moans and cries filled the greenhouse.

"Wait, there's something beneath me," she said at one point.

"Easily fixed," he said as he rolled so she was on top.

"So gentlemanly," she murmured.

He gazed up at her like she was the last woman on earth.

"So smart," he whispered and kissed her again.

They laughed and loved until Clovis landed on Jamie's chest with an angry squawk.

"Damn bird," he said trying to get her off.

"She's jealous."

"She should be. She's not even in the running."

Davis grabbed her and tucked Clovis under her arm. She looked down at Jamie and knew she was stuck. Stuck in love.

Chapter Forty-Three

JAMIE

He was going to die. Not someday. Not hypothetically. Not dramatically in a hunting accident like his sisters predicted.

No. Right now. Tonight. In this bedroom.

Jamie would be killed by dancing or, more accurately, trying to dance.

He froze mid-step, staring at the laptop balanced on his dresser as a man on the screen slid across a ballroom floor like gravity was optional.

Jamie looked down at his own feet.

His left boot pointed east. His right pointed, not east. He was ninety percent sure one ankle had disowned him.

The instructor on the video smiled warmly. "Let's try it together!"

"Let's not," Jamie muttered.

But he did it anyway because he wasn't a coward, at least, not usually. And definitely not when it came to Davis.

He tried the step again.

Right foot back. Left foot sideways? Or was sideways only for foxtrot? Christ, he'd already forgotten.

The instructor glided effortlessly.

Jamie swiveled and kicked the bed frame.

"Son of a—!"

The chicken downstairs squawked in response.

Jamie pressed his hands over his face.

This was humiliating on a spiritual level.

He'd always thought dancing was one of those universal human skills, like walking or sitting or not screaming at jars that seal themselves. But no. Apparently, he had a fatal rhythm deficiency. Musical dyslexia. A tragic case of two left feet, except one of his seemed to be a right foot that had given up on life.

The worst part?

He couldn't let Davis know.

She'd laughed in the greenhouse earlier, the happiest he'd seen her in days. And when she told him she didn't want to mess up the estate, he'd been one thousand percent on board. He wanted to protect that spark in her. All of it. Even the parts she tried to hide.

She cared so damn much.

He wanted to be good enough for her.

And that stupid dancing message from her uncle was mocking him now.

He restarted the video.

"Gentlemen, posture is key. Stand tall, chest open, shoulders relaxed."

He wasn't sure about chest open but he attempted it.

His spine cracked like an old barn door.

"Relaxed," he said through clenched teeth. "Very relaxed. Totally normal."

The instructor continued: "Now lead your partner with confidence. A firm, steady hand."

Jamie lifted his arm.

It trembled. Like he'd just escaped the world's coldest lake.

"Great," he muttered. "I'm going to lead Davis straight into the punch bowl."

He tried the hand position again, imagining Davis standing there smiling at him like he wasn't a man falling apart at the seams.

His chest tightened instead of opening.

Dancing with Davis wouldn't be the problem. The closeness, the smell of her hair, the way she looked up at him like she actually liked him. No, it was everything else. Stubbing his toe, trampling her feet, falling face first into the orchestra. There were serious consequences to his dance interpretation of an elephant.

He wasn't prepared for any of it. Dancing scared him more than any hunt ever had.

He tried the steps again.

Forward. Back. Side. Turn.

Then.

Wham.

His foot caught on the corner of the rug. He went down like a felled elk, arms flailing, dignity gone. He hit the floor with a thud that rattled his teeth and possibly his soul.

Silence followed.

Then the video instructor cheerfully announced:

"Remember. Dancing should feel natural and enjoyable!"

Jamie groaned into the carpet.

Natural. Enjoyable. Sure. And so was dental surgery.

He rolled onto his back and stared at the ceiling, considering every life choice that had led him here. He could shoot a moving target at fifty yards. He could track an injured buck through a snowstorm. He could build a shelter, split firewood, and survive in the cold wilderness with only a knife and a canteen.

But he couldn't dance.

And he couldn't bear the thought of Davis knowing that or even worse dancing with another man because he couldn't do the steps with her. Not after she'd looked at him today like he was more than some stubborn hunter who mucked up her greenhouse and panicked at the sound of sealing jars.

He sighed and sat up.

"Again," he told himself.

His legs protested.

"Again," he repeated, louder, like maybe volume would threaten his feet into obedience.

He restarted the video a fifth time. And a sixth.

On attempt number seven, he successfully completed four steps without injury.

On attempt number eight, he punched the air in victory.

On attempt number nine, he fell sideways into the night-stand, knocking over a lamp.

The bulb shattered.

"Fantastic," he muttered. "At this rate I'll break every object I own before I even make it to the dance floor."

He flopped back on the bed, arms outstretched, sweat sticking his shirt to his skin.

He wanted to quit. He really, really did.

But then he imagined Davis in that stunning red dress. She'd be laughing, glowing, looking like something out of a dream, and imagined her slipping her hand into his.

Trusting him to lead.

Wanting him to.

And something stubborn rose in his chest.

He wasn't letting her down.

"Okay," he said to no one. "Round ten. Bring it."

He stood. He faced the laptop. He braced for war.

"Let's dance, you smug bastard."

The instructor smiled warmly.

Jamie scowled back.

Chapter Forty-Four

DAVIS

The estate had a cleaning crew and a grounds person. They went all out with decorations inside and out for the holidays. The house never felt so alive. Every window glowed with sparkles of lights, and the polished wood floors gleamed. The air buzzed. Anticipation, nerves, maybe a little magic played inside the house.

Davis felt it humming under her skin as she stood in front of the antique mirror in her room, trying not to gape at herself. The red gown fit like someone had designed it for her bones. Structured bodice. Full, swirling skirt. A neckline that managed to be both elegant and faintly sinful.

She lifted the hem and exhaled. "Okay," she told her reflection. "Don't fall down the stairs. That's goal number one."

Goal number two involved not having a meltdown when Jamie saw her. Because she knew, deep in her stubborn, traitorous chest, that she wanted him to see her a certain way.

Wanted him to look at her the way he looked at freshly harvested tomatoes: surprised, impressed, slightly scared.

She grabbed her phone.

Davis: Ready.

Davis: But if you're planning to wear camouflage to the charity ball, tell me now so I can emotionally prepare.

She waited.

Three seconds. Five. Ten.

Her phone buzzed.

Jamie: I'm not wearing camo.

Jamie: Probably.

Jamie: Just come downstairs.

She smirked. Typical.

She slipped into her shoes, deep red heels, just high enough to be dangerous, and stepped from her room. The hallway was quiet except for the soft tick of the grandfather clock.

Her stomach fluttered.

Ridiculous.

She gripped the ivy wrapped banister and descended slowly, one step at a time, hearing the swish of her dress echo through the vast foyer.

Then she saw him.

Oh my my!

Jamie stood at the foot of the stairs, hands clasped behind his back like he wasn't sure what to do with them. The tuxedo fit him too well for comfort. Broad shoulders, crisp lines, and a black tie that made him look devastatingly handsome.

But more than any of those, it was his face. He'd shaved off his beard and she was having trouble coming to terms with her hunting alpha-man versus this straightlaced, respectable man.

He glanced up.

Jamie

He stopped breathing.

Actually. Stopped. Breathing.

She reached the bottom step.

"You look—" He swallowed, straightened, tried again. "You look incredible."

Heat rose up her neck. "Thank you. You're beautiful," she said staring at his clean jaw.

"Beautiful?" He lifted a brow. "This suit is the most uncomfortable fabric prison I've ever stepped into."

"Fashion hurts," she said.

"I'm aware." He gave her a once-over. Not crude, not lingering, but appreciative. Then his gaze caught on hers and warmth flickered between them.

Her pulse fluttered.

He offered his arm. "Ready?"

She hesitated a beat too long. Then slid her hand into the crook of his elbow, feeling the warmth of him beneath the stiff fabric.

"Ready," she said softly.

But when she took the first step forward, he stayed planted, staring at her again like she'd short-circuited an important part of his brain.

"What?" she asked, self-consciousness rising.

Jamie shook his head slowly. "Nothing. Just." His voice dropped. "I knew you'd look beautiful. I just didn't know it would hit like this."

Her breath caught.

She tried to laugh it off even though it was the perfect thing for him to say. "Well. Try not to faint. I'm not carrying you to the car."

"You'd try," he said, lips twitching. "You're stubborn enough."

"You're impossible."

"You're distracting."

They stood there, suspended in the warm glow of sparkling Christmas lights, her dress catching the sparks, while her eyes softened in a way that made him feel warm all over.

The world outside could wait. The ball could wait. Everything could wait.

Jamie cleared his throat, breaking the moment. "Okay," he said, offering a reluctant half-smile. "Now we can go."

They walked toward the door together, her dress sweeping across the floor, his arm steady beneath her hand and neither of them noticed the lights flicker softly behind them, as if the old estate approved.

The hired town car waited, polished so brightly it reflected the glow of the mansion's windows. The driver stood beside the back door like a statue, dipped his head to them, and held it open.

Jamie helped Davis inside, careful of her dress, careful of everything. She seemed to be made of moonlight and silk. He slid in beside her, the door closing with a soft thump that sealed them into warm leather, hushed lighting, and the faint scent of cedar.

The engine purred.

Jamie adjusted his tie, muttering under his breath.

Davis glanced at him, then did a very slow, very deliberate double take.

He stiffened. "What?"

She bit her lip, which was not helpful for his concentration. "So. The beard."

He grimaced. "What about it?"

"It's gone."

"Yes."

"Completely gone."

"I'm aware," he said tightly.

Her lips curved into a wickedly delighted smile. "You look younger."

"Good younger or bad younger?"

She pretended to contemplate. "Hmm. Somewhere between 'responsible adult' and 'guy who just got carded buying cough syrup.'"

He groaned. "Fantastic."

She scooted a fraction closer, barely an inch, but enough that he felt the shift. Her skirt brushed his leg. Her floral perfume moved with her.

"I mean," she added, "you look so different."

He narrowed his eyes. "Different how?"

"Less rugged hunter, more polished gentleman. And beautiful." Her hand came out and her fingers ran across his jaw. "Your face is so smooth. It's weird."

He ran a hand over his chin self-consciously. "I hate it."

"It's incredible."

"It's drafty."

Davis snorted, then slapped a hand over her mouth, embarrassed.

Jamie slumped back. "My chin has never been this exposed to the elements. I'm defenseless. Vulnerable. Like a newborn fawn."

The driver coughed violently. Possibly choking. Possibly suppressing laughter.

Davis leaned closer, voice dropping. "I do like seeing your jawline. It's a good jaw. Very sharp."

Jamie's pulse jumped. "Sharp?"

"Mmhmm." Her fingers touched his cheek again. "You look, now don't get cocky, very clean and very kiss—"

She cut herself off, eyes widening.

Jamie blinked. "Very what?"

"Nothing."

"It didn't sound like nothing."

"It was definitely nothing."

The driver's shoulders shook.

Jamie tried and failed not to smirk. "If you're saying my face is kissable without the beard—"

"I'm not saying that."

"But you were going to."

She crossed her arms, cheeks warming. "You asked me for honesty. Don't make me regret it."

"You think I look kissable."

"I will literally throw myself out of this moving vehicle."

The driver, bless his soul, raised the partition halfway, pretending to do them both a mercy.

Jamie leaned slightly toward her, voice low but amused. "Well, since we're being honest, you look—"

"No," she said quickly. "Don't. You'll make it worse."

He tilted his head. "Worse for you or for me?"

Her eyes flicked to his bare jaw, then away again, fast. "That depends," she muttered.

God help him, he loved her fluster, her fire, her attempts to hide behind sarcasm that didn't quite work.

She moved away from him slightly and he rested his hand near hers on the seat. "For the record," he said softly, "beard or no beard, I wanted to look good for you tonight."

Her breath caught.

The car hummed through the twilight.

He took her hand.

She didn't move at all, really, except for the small, barely-there smile that curved at the corner of her mouth.

"Jamie?" she whispered.

"Yeah?"

"You do look very kissable but I don't want to ruin my makeup."

And if the driver didn't suddenly roll that privacy partition all the way up, it was only because he didn't want to miss anything.

Jamie moved in close like he was going to kiss her anyway. "Good. I have the same problem and I didn't bring touch up makeup with me."

Chapter Forty-Five

DAVIS

The ballroom shone with thousands of Christmas lights. It was dazzling and there was no other word for it. Dozens of chandeliers shimmered like constellations suspended from the ceiling, each casting warm, glittering light across the polished floor. Candlelit wreaths traced the windows, and garlands draped from balcony rails with the delicate touch of snow dust. Musicians tuned soft notes that floated through the air like drifting snowflakes.

It felt like stepping into a snow globe. It was a world Davis wasn't sure she belonged in until tonight.

Because Jamie stepped in beside her. And, somehow, that made everything easier.

People turned. Heads swiveled. Conversations hiccuped mid-sentence.

It was obvious that no one knew who they were, but they were too polite to ask.

Her red dress swept the floor in waves of silk, catching the sparkling light, and Jamie's devastating tuxedo made him look like he'd stepped out of a magazine spread titled *Men Who Have No Right Looking That Good After Complaining About Canning.*

He offered her his arm again, and she took it to keep herself steady.

"You okay?" he murmured, leaning close.

"Fine," she whispered back. "You?"

He exhaled. "No idea."

She smiled.

They moved through the crowd, accepting greetings, handshakes, compliments, all while Jamie hovered close, but not possessively. Just there. A solid anchor in a sea of glitter.

She didn't miss the looks he got either. And she definitely noticed the way his clean-shaven jawline made women do double-takes.

She bumped his arm lightly. "You're causing distractions."

He dipped his head. "Just trying to blend in."

"You're failing."

"Thank you."

She covered a laugh with her champagne glass.

The string quartet eased into a soft, lilting melody, romantic but not overwhelming. The kind of music that tugged gently at your ribs and whispered, *Come dance.*

She looked at him, somehow knowing he didn't dance. She didn't want him to feel bad so she tried to keep the longing off her face as she watched partners take the floor.

Jamie

He stiffened.

Here it was.

The moment she'd been waiting for.

The moment he'd been dreading.

She turned to him, expecting his usual deflection, something like "Let's get snacks instead" or "The floor's too shiny; it's a hazard."

Instead, he inhaled deeply.

Looked at her.

And held out his hand.

"Dance with me?"

Her breath caught. "Jamie, are you sure?"

"No," he said honestly. "But I want to."

She placed her hand in his.

He led her onto the floor.

Jamie had faced down charging boars with more confidence.

But when Davis stepped into his arms, soft red silk brushing his legs, her hand threading into his, her other resting lightly on his shoulder, something inside him unfurled.

She smelled like winter apples along with her floral perfume. Her eyes lifted to his. The world stopped.

He remembered the videos. He remembered the steps. Right foot back. Left to the side. Guide gently. Lead confidently. Don't crush her feet.

He started moving.

Holy hell.

It worked. He wasn't tripping. He wasn't stomping. His legs weren't rebelling against him like unionized chickens.

They were actually, inexplicably, dancing.

Davis blinked up at him. "Jamie."

He tensed. "I'm stepping on your dress, aren't I? I swear I'm not trying to."

"No," she whispered. "You're good."

He almost missed a step. Almost.

"Good?" he repeated, dumbstruck. "Like, passable-good or actual-good?"

She leaned in closer, smiling against his shoulder. "Good-good."

A disbelieving laugh escaped him.

He guided her through a turn. She trusted him completely, letting the skirt flare around them like wine spilling onto moonlight. Her hand tightened in his.

The music swelled. Their bodies found a rhythm that felt older than the dance instructor on the video. When he turned her again, she twirled effortlessly in his arms, breathless.

"Where did this come from?" she murmured.

He hesitated.

Her eyebrow arched.

He sighed. "I maybe, might have, sort of practiced."

"Practiced?"

"At home."

She blinked at him. "You practiced dancing."

"Yes."

"In your bedroom."

"Yes."

"By yourself."

"Yes." Then, quickly, "Do not picture that."

She laughed with no restraint.

The couple beside them glanced over, smiling as if they could feel the joy radiating off her.

Jamie felt like he'd swallowed every chandelier in the room.

He pulled her gently closer.

Her cheek brushed his jaw. His breath shivered.

"I wanted to get this right," he murmured into her hair.

Her steps faltered for half a heartbeat.

Then she whispered, "You got it perfect."

Song after song, they stayed on the floor.

He led. She followed. They breathed to the same rhythm.

All around them, the ballroom sparkled and shimmered on the polished floors, the quartet's music threading through air scented with winter greenery, laughter, soft conversation, and the whisper of silk.

It was a night they would remember for reasons neither dared say out loud.

And when the final notes faded, Davis lifted her chin, eyes shining.

"You," she said softly, "are full of surprises."

Jamie exhaled with a helpless half-smile.

"You have no idea."

Chapter Forty-Six

DAVIS

The world looked dipped in powdered sugar. The estate grounds were blanketed in fresh snow, untouched except for one very questionable set of footprints leading in zigzags from the barn. Davis chose not to investigate that mystery before coffee.

Inside, the house was magical. Garland wrapped the banisters. Candles flickered in frosted glass. The scent of cinnamon and cloves drifted from the kitchen, though that was less "holiday magic" and more Jamie burning something and opening every window to hide the evidence.

It was cozy. Warm. A little chaotic.

Perfect.

It had taken them a few days after the ball to find the perfect tree to cut and decorate. It was the best run up to Christmas that Davis remembered in her life.

She padded downstairs in fuzzy socks, flannel pajamas, and hair pulled into a loose bun that barely survived sleep. She'd promised herself she would not overthink things this morning. Not the ball. Not the dancing. Not the way Jamie had held her like she was something he didn't want to let go of. Nope. No overthinking at all because it's all she'd done since the ball.

She stepped into the living room.

Jamie was on the floor under the tree wrestling a ribbon off a box while a chicken sat on top of it like royalty overseeing a subject.

"Morning," Davis said.

Jamie startled, then tried to pretend he hadn't.

"Hey," he said casually, still prying ribbon from under a very determined hen. "Merry Christmas."

"Merry Christmas." She walked closer, eyes narrowing. "Is that a gift for Clovis?"

"No." He paused. "Maybe."

Clovis clucked proudly.

Davis crossed her arms. "We said we weren't exchanging gifts for the chicken."

"We didn't say that."

"We heavily implied it."

"You implied it," he corrected. "I disagreed."

"You disagreed by pretending you couldn't hear me."

"I genuinely couldn't. You were in the pantry and the blender was on."

She snorted. "Fine. But why does the chicken need a gift?"

Clovis pecked Jamie's sleeve.

"Because," he said, "she's been through a lot of trauma in her young life. And she brings joy. And she's been cold since it snowed."

Davis softened despite her best efforts. "You're ridiculous."

"Thank you." He pushed the chicken's fluffy butt off the gift, freeing it. "Anyway, this is hers."

Davis eyed the shape suspiciously. "What is it?"

"I'll show you if you don't laugh."

"No promises."

He peeled off the paper.

It was a chicken sweater.

Red and white stripes. Tiny, knitted sleeves. A miniature pom-pom on the hood.

Davis blinked. "Oh my God."

"Don't laugh," he warned.

"I'm not laughing," she said, voice wobbling.

Clovis, however, clucked in horror.

"She'll wear it," Jamie insisted trying to strangle her into it. "Eventually. Maybe. If we bribe her."

"With what?" Davis asked. "Worm-flavored macarons?"

"Don't tempt me," he said seriously as the bird twisted and clucked.

Clovis finally flapped away, offended.

Jamie sighed. "She doesn't appreciate my generosity."

Davis grinned. "Actually, she might. Because, well," She stepped to the tree and plucked a small, wrapped box from under it. "This is for her too."

Jamie's eyebrows shot up. "You got my chicken a gift."

"It's different."

"It is not different."

"It's completely different."

"It's exactly the same."

She thrust the box at him. "Just open it."

He unwrapped it.

Inside was a tiny chicken tiara. A sparkly, gold, very elegant, chicken tiara.

Jamie stared at it. "This is objectively worse."

"It's festive."

"It's deranged."

"Clovis will love it."

Clovis strutted back into the room like she owned the house and maybe the world.

Jamie held the tiara toward her. She pecked it instantly.

Davis squealed. "See? She loves it!"

"She's trying to kill it."

"Same thing."

Jamie cleared his throat after propping the darned thing on the chick's head and reached under the tree again. "Okay. Human gifts now. This one's for you."

Davis's stomach fluttered.

She unwrapped it slowly. Inside was a small wooden hand-carved box. When she opened it, her breath hitched.

A delicate necklace lay inside. Silver. With a tiny charm shaped like a basil leaf.

She looked up at him. "Jamie."

He rubbed the back of his neck. "I figured you'd hate anything too flashy. And, I don't know, you like the greenhouse. And you laugh when basil sticks to you. And it made me think of you."

Her heart melted into a sentimental puddle.

"It's perfect," she whispered.

He gave a devastating smile.

She cleared her throat before she did something embarrassing like kiss him in front of a jealous chicken.

"Okay," she said, "your turn."

She handed him a slim, square package. He opened it carefully.

Inside was a sleek, leather-bound field journal.

He ran his thumb over the embossed initials on the front. "DTR?" he asked.

"Dumb Things Jamie Records," she said.

He snorted. "Try again."

"Daily Tracking & Reflection," she offered. "For hunting. Or farming. Or, I don't know, dancing practice."

His ears turned pink. "You're never letting that go, are you?"

"Not a chance."

He opened the journal and found the note she'd tucked inside:

For the man who keeps surprising me and should write down the things he's too stubborn to say out loud.

He swallowed.

Hard.

"Davis," he said quietly.

And suddenly the room felt very small, very warm, and very full of unspoken things.

He reached for her hand.

She let him take it.

Neither moved for a long moment.

Then, a loud cluck shattered the spell.

Clovis launched herself onto Jamie's knee, wearing the tiara crookedly and glaring like she gave a royal decree regarding Christmas breakfast.

Davis burst out laughing.

Jamie groaned.

"Fine," he said. "Food first."

The day couldn't have been more perfect and Davis went all out for Christmas dinner. She proudly stood over her feast when Jamie walked into the kitchen to help her carry it to the table.

"Go-Furkey," she said proudly.

He looked at the glob of whatever it was made from. "Do I have a choice?"

"Nope."

"Then Merry Christmas to me."

The Go-Furkey sat on the table like something sculpted by a chef with emotional baggage. But Davis had basted it with a rosemary glaze, roasted it with vegetables, and smiled the whole way through dinner, so Jamie pretended it was delicious.

Actually, it kind of was.

They ate. They laughed. They stole glances at each other across the candlelit table.

Clovis fell asleep in her sweater and tiara on a chair like a tiny drunk queen.

When dessert came, apple crisp and whipped coconut cream, Jamie reached across the table, brushed a crumb from Davis's lip, and said softly, "Merry Christmas, Davis."

Her heart went warm.

"Merry Christmas, Jamie."

The house creaked gently. Snow fell outside. And for the first time since they arrived at the estate, the place didn't feel big or strange or overwhelming.

It felt like home.

Chapter Forty-Seven

DAVIS

Spring arrived like it had been holding its breath all winter. The snow melted, leaving behind dark, rich soil that hummed with rebirth. Tiny green shoots appeared in the garden beds. Wildflowers popped up along the gravel drive as if the earth had decided it was done being gloomy. Even the greenhouse felt sun-warm in the afternoons.

And inside the house, something had changed too.

The air felt fuller. Happier. Lived in.

Their coats hung together on the hooks by the door. His boots and her rain clogs lined up like mismatched soldiers. A chicken, who now owned three sweaters and one tiara, occasionally patrolled the hallway carpet like she was on a fashion runway.

Davis still wasn't sure when this stopped being her uncle's house and started being their home.

Maybe it happened the night of the charity ball. Maybe Christmas dinner. Maybe the day Jamie rebuilt the greenhouse door without being asked, humming off-key while she pretended not to watch him.

Or maybe it was today.

April first.

One year since she'd strode into this place with a box of belongings, a heart full of questions, and no idea what she was walking into.

She stood on the porch now, hands wrapped around a mug of chamomile tea, breathing in the scent of thawed earth and blooming flowers. Birds called to each other from the branches. The morning sun glowed on the horizon.

Soon she would tear into the greenhouse again and start the planting cycle once more. She couldn't wait.

Behind her, the front door opened.

Jamie stepped out, hair still damp from his shower, wearing jeans and a faded blue t-shirt that fit him unfairly well. He carried two envelopes, one thin, one thick.

"Morning," he said, voice gravelly-warm.

"Morning."

He handed her the knitted sweater she always forgot to grab. "It's chilly," he said.

She took it, savoring the brush of his fingers. "Thank you."

He smiled softly, then held up the envelopes.

"I collected these before I took my shower. They were in the mailbox."

Davis frowned. "Both?"

"Yeah." He flexed the thicker one. "From the solicitor's office."

He lifted the thinner. "And this one has your uncle's handwriting."

Her breath stopped.

Handwriting she'd only seen on letters delivered at the strangest, most inconvenient times. Letters she'd dreaded and needed in equal measure. And now, the last one.

"Oh," she whispered.

Jamie watched her carefully. "You okay?"

She nodded automatically, even though the air felt suddenly tight in her chest.

He stepped closer, lowering his voice. "Davis, we don't have to open them right now."

But she did.

She could feel it. Today wasn't random. She'd learned that her Uncle Anthony never did anything without meaning. April first wasn't just a date. It was *the* date.

The day everything changed.

The day they inherited the house. The day she inherited Jamie and had no idea what it would mean.

She swallowed. "I want to open it now."

"Okay," he said softly.

Davis slid her thumb under the flap.

The paper inside was folded twice, neatly. She unfolded it, hands trembling just slightly.

Her uncle's handwriting curled across the page.

My Dearest Davis and Jamie,

If you are reading this, it has been one year since you first stepped into the place I loved most in the world. One year since I trusted you both to bring it back to life.

Homes are not built by stone or lumber. They are built by the people willing to love them.

And I knew you would. I also knew you could not do it alone. By now, the estate has chosen its keepers. I hope you have allowed yourselves to choose, too.

In the larger envelope, you will find the final deed, as well as one last request.

Not an obligation.

A blessing.

Live here. Truly live. Cultivate not just the greenhouse, but your own hearts. Laugh often. Stay brave. Let yourselves be loved.

This house belongs to you both. Its future is yours. And if all has gone as I hoped, you are no longer alone.

Uncle Anthony

Davis stared at the letter.

Birdsong filled the quiet.

Her throat tightened, tears burning behind her eyes in a way she didn't want to fight anymore.

Jamie touched her back gently. "Davis."

She didn't turn around. She couldn't. Her voice trembled. "He knew."

"Knew what?" Jamie asked softly.

She exhaled, shakily. "That we'd..." She waved vaguely between them, helpless. "That we'd become whatever this is."

He didn't answer at first. Just stepped in front of her, gently cupping her cheek so she had to look at him.

"Whatever this is," he echoed, "is the best damn thing I never saw coming."

Her heart flipped.

He brushed a tear from her cheek with his thumb. "Hey. Don't cry."

"I'm not crying," she whispered.

"You're definitely crying."

"I'm emotionally leaking."

He smiled that slow, warm Jamie-smile that always unraveled her. "Better?" he asked.

She huffed out a laugh, but her eyes were still wet. "I can't believe this is the last letter."

"It's not," he murmured. "Not really."

"What do you mean?"

He held up the thick envelope from the solicitor. "This one's from him too. Papers, probably. Instructions. A plan."

"A plan?"

"Maybe," he said. "But we don't have to open it yet."

She blinked. "Why not?"

He took the letter from her hands and set it gently on the porch railing.

"Because it's our anniversary," he said softly. "One year in this house. One year surviving chickens and exploding canning jars and this thing happening between us." His eyes held hers. "I want a good memory before anything else changes."

Her breath caught. "What kind of memory?"

"The kind," he said, stepping closer, "that you don't need a letter to understand."

Her heart pounded.

He lifted a hand to her cheek. The morning sun warmed her back. The scent of earth and lilacs rose around them. Clovis clucked somewhere in the distance, deeply offended for reasons unknown.

Then Jamie went to one knee, holding a ring in one hand.

"I love you. Will you marry me Davis Jules Bernard?"

Her entire life flashed before her eyes.

She was so madly in love and she read the reciprocal love in his gaze.

"Yes," she said breathlessly.

Jamie stood and kissed her.

Soft at first. Then deeper when her lips answered him without hesitation.

The world melted. Spring air, sunlight, birdcall, memory, hope, all folding into one impossibly beautiful moment.

When they finally pulled apart, breath combining with breath, Jamie whispered,

"Happy anniversary, Davis," and he slipped the ring on her finger.

She leaned her forehead to his, smiling through tears as she admired the perfect solitaire diamond.

"Happy anniversary, Jamie."

He swooped her into his arms and carried her into the house.

And behind them on the porch railing, the unopened envelope waited.

Chapter Forty-Eight

DAVIS

The house woke slowly. Early light poured through the tall windows, soft and golden, catching floating dust motes and warming the wooden floors.

Davis stirred first.

For a moment, she didn't move, just lay there, cocooned in warmth, replaying the previous day in a soft, dizzy loop.

Jamie's hand in hers. The feeling she had when he asked her to marry him. And then his mouth on hers. And his arms around her. And—

She cut her own thoughts off before they drifted into steamy romance-novel territory.

Beside her, Jamie breathed deeply, still asleep, still holding her like she might disappear if he let go. His face, incredibly handsome, annoyingly kissable, was relaxed in a way she rarely saw.

Davis ran a thumb along his knuckles.

The porch. The unopened letter. It waited for them downstairs.

Her chest tightened. Not with fear, but with something she hadn't felt in years.

Possibility.

Jamie shifted and murmured, "Stop staring at me. It's creepy."

She jumped. "You were awake!"

"Barely," he said, eyes still closed, "but even unconscious I can feel judgment."

"You proposed to me yesterday and I have the ring to prove it." She nudged him. "I'm allowed to stare."

He cracked one eye open. "Not if you're cataloging my flaws."

"I was appreciating your face," she said, deadpan.

"Oh." He blinked. "Well. Carry on."

She laughed and pushed his shoulder. "Get up. We have something to read."

His expression sobered instantly.

"Yeah," he said. "We do."

They wrapped themselves in a shared blanket, half because it was still chilly, half because neither wanted to let go of the other, and stepped outside.

The porch boards creaked under their bare feet. A faint breeze carried the scent of wet soil and new grass. The unopened envelope still rested on the railing exactly where Jamie left it.

Waiting.

Davis reached for it.

Jamie's hand covered hers. "Do you want me to open it?"

She shook her head. "No. I need to do this."

He nodded.

She slid her thumb under the flap and removed the papers inside.

The first page was simple.

The Deed:

Gables Estate — Granted in Full to Davis Jules Harland & James Luke Callaway

Her breath caught.

Jamie leaned closer.

Then, below their names, a handwritten note in her uncle's looping script:

Because a home built by two hearts is stronger than any legacy left by one.

Davis blinked hard against the sudden sting in her eyes.

Jamie touched her back lightly. "Hey," he murmured. "I've got you."

She nodded and turned the page.

The next sheets detailed accounts, investments, trust holdings. Zeros. Lots of zeros.

More than she had ever imagined.

Jamie let out a very quiet, very stunned, "Holy hell."

She exhaled shakily. "He left everything. Everything he ever built."

"To us," Jamie said softly.

"To us." She handed him the page.

Jamie looked at her, something intense flickering behind his eyes. "Davis, this is life changing."

"I know."

"It's freedom."

"I know."

"It's opportunity."

"I know." Her voice wobbled. "I just... I don't know what he expected us to do with all this."

Jamie gently pulled the rest of the papers from the envelope.

The final page was another handwritten note.

He read it aloud.

My dear Davis, and to the man who will stand beside you,

If you are reading this, then the estate is no longer mine, but yours.

I trust you both to choose a future worthy of it. I leave you this fortune not as a burden, but as a gift of freedom. Build something. Save something. Protect something. Create something beautiful.

This house thrives when laughter fills its halls and when its land is tended by hearts that care more for people than for profit. I was a curmudgeon and allowed my hopes and dreams to dwindle after my wife died. Don't do that. Use this inheritance however you choose but use it. Grow the gardens. Restore the orchards. Open the estate to others. Or simply live here with joy.

But do not be afraid to dream recklessly.

With love,

Anthony

Davis pressed a hand to her mouth. The tears came anyway.

Jamie wrapped his arms around her, pulling her against his chest.

She breathed him in and let the tears fall.

"He trusted us," she whispered.

"He did," Jamie murmured. "And he was right."

She shook her head. "Jamie, I know the dream I want for this house but I don't know if you'll want it too."

"You don't need to worry about that. I know you and I can picture your dream. Our dream," he said. "Together."

She pulled back slightly, looking up at him. His hair was tousled from sleep. His eyes were impossibly gentle.

"Together?" she echoed.

He smiled slowly. "We're engaged, aren't we? I think that means we're doing everything together now."

Her heart squeezed.

Clovis strutted onto the porch wearing her spring sweater, looking like a fuzzy feathered judge of important matters.

Jamie groaned. "Great. She's here to weigh in."

Davis laughed through her tears. "She wants to help."

"With what?" he asked.

"Dreaming recklessly."

Clovis clucked as if in agreement.

Jamie exhaled, shaking his head. "Okay then. Three of us. Fine."

He pressed a kiss to Davis's forehead. "This place will make a huge difference in animal lives," he said.

Davis nodded, emotion blooming warm in her chest. "*We* will," she said quietly. And Jamie did know exactly what she had planned.

He pulled her in and kissed her.

Chapter Forty-Nine

DAVIS

They stood together looking at Uncle Tony's head-stone that finally rested in the small family graveyard behind the house. You could see just the corner of the greenhouse from here, which made Davis happy. She liked it that her uncle was near the building he loved.

The headstone was simple with his name and the year he was born and then died. His wife rested beside him on one side with Davis and Lawrence on the other.

"We'll rest here one day," Jamie said softly.

"Bite your tongue. I'm being turned into a tree. The tree can be planted here but I won't harm nature with my death."

Jamie rolled his eyes.

"I saw that."

"I'm sure you did. Do I have any say over how and where I'm buried?" he asked cautiously.

"Of course you do, honey. You'll come to my way of thinking and that way we won't need to argue about it."

"That's what I thought would happen."

She placed her arm through his. "We need to pack."

"We need to, something," he said and kissed her. "It is our second anniversary."

They ended up racing to the house and tugging off clothing as they ran. It was another hour before they finished packing and left for the airport.

The heat pressed down like a living thing. Not unbearable, just full of sun and dust and the wild heartbeat of Africa. Davis wiped a line of sweat from her temple as the open-air jeep crawled along the dry earth track.

Acacia trees dotted the savanna. A warm wind carried the herbal scent of scrubland and something that made her chest tighten with awe.

Jamie raised his binoculars again.

"Movement," he murmured. "North ridge."

Davis leaned forward, pulse quickening. "Rhino?"

"Pretty sure."

Her heart squeezed with reverence. They'd spent months preparing for this. Weeks studying the terrain. Days training with specialists. And even now, after all that, Davis still couldn't believe she was here. That they were here.

A far cry from tomato bombs in a greenhouse. A lifetime away from tension-filled canning jars and chickens in sweaters. A millennia away from hunting wild animals as trophies.

The jeep hummed to a stop. The guide, Thabo, pointed down the slope. "There. By the brush line. Young male."

Jamie exhaled slowly, steadying his breathing. His posture shifted, focused the way she remembered from his old hunting days, but even more purposeful now.

They climbed out quietly.

The earth warmed her boots. The wind pressed her shirt against her back. Somewhere in the distance, birds called to each other, and another animal snorted near a watering hole.

Jamie checked the rifle.

Davis checked her stomach.

"Still okay?" he whispered.

She nodded. "Still okay."

This was the life they chose. This was the only kind of "hunt" they participated in.

Davis followed Jamie through the brush. Thabo stayed at their side, scanning for movement, gauging wind direction. Sweat beaded on Jamie's temple but his hand didn't shake.

They'd turned the Gables Estate into a farm sanctuary, home for rescue animals, abandoned livestock, orphaned goats, injured wildlife, and one chicken who ruled them all. It was still a work in progress but they were making headway steadily.

They crested the ridge.

And there he was.

A young rhino. Massive, magnificent, grazing near a patch of shade. His hide glimmered in the sun like armor forged by the earth itself. His horn curved proudly from his nose. A target for men with greed and death in their hearts.

Davis felt her throat tighten.

Thabo whispered, "The poachers have already scoped him out. We found tracks last night."

Jamie's jaw ticked.

She placed her hand on his back to steady him. "Whenever you're ready," she whispered.

Jamie raised the rifle.

A long breath in. A slow breath out. Silence.

Then, *thffft*.

The dart sailed through the hot air, the tiniest whisper of sound. It struck the rhino's flank cleanly. The animal jolted. Snorted. Stumbled.

Davis held her breath.

Thabo counted quietly under his breath. "Three, two, one."

The rhino's legs buckled gently, and he lowered himself to the ground.

Davis exhaled shakily, emotion flooding her chest.

Jamie lowered the rifle.

"You did good," she whispered.

"No," he said softly, watching the majestic creature breathe, "we did good."

Reserve workers rushed in from their positions, carrying medical kits and saws designed not for harm, but preservation. In minutes, they were at the rhino's side, working efficiently, cutting away the horn that poachers would kill him for, taking blood samples and getting a tag ready.

Saving his life.

Davis crouched near the rhino's massive head, placing her hand gently on his leathery skin. "You're safe," she whispered. "We've got you."

Jamie knelt beside her, resting a steady hand on her back.

The workers finished. The horn was placed in a secure lockbox. When the rhino woke, he would rise lighter, unaware of the human evils he'd been saved from.

Jamie let out a slow breath, eyes shining with something deep.

He kissed her hair. "Your uncle would've loved this."

She smiled. "He would've loved you too."

Jamie huffed a small laugh. "Even with the beard?"

"Especially *without* the beard," she teased.

They stayed like that, kneeling beside a creature spared from cruelty, the African sun warming their backs, spring wind threading through the grass, until Thabo called to them with a grin.

"Good work, you two. That bull has a real shot now."

Davis took Jamie's hand as they stood.

A sanctuary in America.

A life built side by side.

Purpose.

Love.

Partnership.

And now saving a majestic animal halfway across the world.

Jamie squeezed her hand gently.

"Ready for the next one?" he asked.

She smiled. "Always."

Together, they walked back toward the jeep, sun at their backs, the future wide open, and the world, at least this small piece of it, a little safer because of them.

Epilogue

The shimmering viewing globe hummed softly as Tony leaned in, squinting at the scene inside.

"Look at them," he said proudly. "My niece Davis finally stopped threatening Jamie with tofu-based punishments."

Lary, lover of chaos, peered over Tony's shoulder. "You would take credit. Even though half of your instructions looked like they were written during a morphine episode."

Tony sniffed. "Genius is often misunderstood."

Behind them, the third member of their eternal trio cleared her throat.

Older Davis, the woman both men had loved in life and still adored in death, crossed her arms. "For the record, I warned you two that naming her after me would cause confusion."

Tony gestured dramatically at the globe. "It's only confusing when you're in the room. Or when someone says, 'Davis is crying,' and we panic."

Lary pointed down at the shimmering vision where younger Davis and Jamie were chasing a runaway chicken through the sanctuary yard. "Well, at least this Davis cries for joyful chicken reasons. Not for 'you two angered another angel' reasons."

Older Davis sighed affectionately. "Please stop harassing the angels."

"You set one on fire," Tony reminded her.

"Yes," she said, smiling. "Because it gave me a hard time and I knew it wouldn't truly burn."

They all turned back to the globe.

Below, younger Davis grabbed Jamie by the shirt and kissed him breathless. The chicken looked away like it was scandalized.

Tony grinned. "See? I told you forcing them to share the estate would fix everything."

Lary elbowed him. "You forced us to share a house once. It did not fix everything."

"It brought us closer together."

"You slept on the roof," Lary said.

Older Davis giggled. "You two were hopeless without me."

The sphere brightened, the view expanding to show Jamie and younger Davis working together beside the sanctuary barn, laughing, muddy, deeply in love.

Older Davis sighed. "I like watching her. She's strong. She's stubborn. She's very me."

"She cooks better," Tony said.

Older Davis glared. "Excuse me?"

Tony coughed. "I mean, she cooks differently."

Lary murmured, "Well, you did once try to sauté a shoe."

"It looked like eggplant," she hissed.

They fell into a companionable silence, the three of them shoulder to shoulder, watching the couple below.

"I wish I could tell her I'm proud of her," older Davis whispered.

"You did," Tony said gently. "In all the ways that mattered."

"And besides," Lary added, tapping the glowing globe proudly, "we're allowed a yearly visitation through this very fancy cosmic bubble thing. Very official. Possibly illegal."

A goat wandered into the greenhouse below.

Jamie groaned.

Younger Davis shouted something involving holy words and unholy hooves.

The three spirits burst out laughing.

"Alright," older Davis said, wiping a tear of mirth, "they'll survive. They've got love, land, a chicken with delusions of royalty, and a goat with good taste in vegetables."

Tony put an arm around her ethereal shoulders. "Just like we did."

Lary clapped them both on the back. "Come on. Who's up for a celestial picnic? I found a cloud shaped like a recliner."

Older Davis beamed. "Only if we can check on them again tonight before the globe goes dark for another year."

"Of course," Tony said.

The globe dimmed to a soft glow behind them as they drifted off, still bickering, still laughing, still in love with the messy, beautiful lives they left behind.

About Holly

Holly S Roberts is an award-winning author which includes appearing on the USA TODAY list multiple times and selling more than one million books worldwide. Max, her Rottweiler, is never far from her side because he listens when she has plot problems and offers rare insights when encouraged with cookies.

www.ingramcontent.com/pod-product-compliance
Lightning Source LLC
Chambersburg PA
CBHW070239200726
48293CB00005B/1691